I0609427

WHISPERED
desire

BLACKCHAPEL BASTARDS

HALLIE
BENNETT

Copyright © 2025 by Hallie Bennett

All rights reserved.
No part of this publication may be reproduced, distributed, or transmitted in any form or by any means, including photocopying, recording, or other electronic or mechanical methods, without the prior written permission of the publisher, except as permitted by U.S. copyright law. For permission requests, contact thearrowedheart@gmail.com. The story, all names, characters, and incidents portrayed in this production are fictitious. No identification with actual persons (living or deceased), places, buildings, and products is intended or should be inferred.

Searching for more obsessed heroes? Check out the Mountain Men of Suitor's Crossing[1] series!

And don't miss out on Hallie Bennett updates by

<u>joining her VIPs</u>[2]!

---

1. https://www.amazon.com/dp/B0BZ3F9GG4

2. https://www.thearrowedheart.com/hallie-bennett

CONTENT NOTES

Suicidal Ideation, Anxiety/Depression, Toxic Family &
Friendships (not between main characters), Violence, Explicit
Sex, Cursing/Offensive Language, Dubious Consent,
Stalking, Light Dom/Sub Dynamic
**This is a fictional story. Love is a powerful healer but is not
a cure-all or substitute for medical professionals.**

GLOSSARY

Dites-leur de nous envoyer les contrats signés avant la fin des activités, sinon l'accord est annulé = Tell them to send the signed contracts to us by end of business or else the deal is off.

Qu'allez-vous faire s'ils ne se conforment pas? = What are you going to do if they don't comply?

Êtes-vous d'accord? = Are you okay?

Es-tu blessé? = Are you injured?

Fille folle = Crazy girl

Ma cherie = My darling

Putain de merde = Fuck

De toutes les bêtises = Of all the silly

C'est ça, mon petit ange = That's right, my little angel

Ton cul parfait est sur le point de me faire jouir. Tu es si belle, ma douce fille = Your perfect ass is about to make me come. You're so beautiful, my sweet girl.

Je suis désolé, mon ange. = I'm sorry, my angel.

Quel plaisir de vous voir = What a delight you are.

Attrape-la! = Grab her!

Boulangerie = Bakery

Je t'aime, mon petit ange. = I love you, my little angel.

Reste avec moi, s'il te plaît, ma douce. Je t'aime. = Stay with me, please, sweet girl. I love you.

GLOSSARY

PREFACE

Once upon a time, seven illegitimate sons of the world's most powerful men arrived at Blackchapel Manor. Young and embittered, the lives they knew were gone forever, to be replaced by one ruthless goal—revenge.

In the thick of the woods, a crumbling stone chapel became their classroom. They didn't learn how to read or write within its cold interior but to torture and kill those who would compromise their mission to destroy the men who fathered then abandoned them.

Named for the dark deeds conducted inside, seven boys became seven men known as the Blackchapel Bastards.

Mathias Beaumont.

Aleksei and Dmitri Petrov.

Luca D'Amora.

Jonah Anderson.

Hugo Steele.

Rafael Vasquez.

Boys who entered Blackchapel orphaned and unskilled.

Until a brotherhood of men emerged—dangerous and craving retribution.

PROLOGUE

MATHIAS BEAUMONT

TWELVE YEARS OLD

"Harder!" Conrad shouts from his position on the cracked altar. Overhead, dozens of tiny black bodies shifted at the disturbance but otherwise remained unaffected. The bats who made their home in the dilapidated chapel eaves had long ago become accustomed to raised voices—whether it was Conrad or one of the many victims he apprehended for these exercises. My fingers tighten around the thin wire in my hands, pain slicing at my palms, and a moment of indecision adds another layer of sweat to my temples. The unlucky man at my mercy gasps and flops around like a wriggling fish, and I'd like nothing more than to release him back to sea—*the greater Boston area*—but I know his fate is sealed.

As is mine.

"Are you going soft on me, Beaumont? Does Hugo need to step in and show you how to properly strangle a man?"

My eyes find Hugo in the shadows. The sun set hours ago, causing the winter chill to deepen within the chapel's decaying walls. I used to wish for it to tumble into a heap on my head—or Conrad's; I wasn't picky. A stony burial befitting the ill deeds committed here.

But the old structure remained standing.

To mock me.

Mock *us*.

The man beneath me lifts his hands to scratch at his throat where the wire digs into the skin and a red line of blood forms. It isn't deep enough to kill him yet. That's why Conrad is annoyed and threatening to have his own son finish the job.

But I refuse to add to Hugo's burden.

It's bad enough that his dad is a fucking psycho whose sole purpose is to train the six bastard sons of his sworn enemies to kill. A sadistic bastard whose lesson tonight is how to strangle a man to death with a piece of wire. I don't even get the luxury of gloves to protect myself from the weapon's sharpness.

"Three, two—"

I tug with all my might and almost collapse in relief when the wire slices through tendons and arteries, shutting off the man's desperate cries, and allowing my labored breathing to rattle through the chapel as Conrad and six other boys stare at the carnage.

"Petrovs. You're up." Conrad claps his hands together and gestures to the chainsaw at his feet. "Chop him up for proper disposal."

Dmitri and Aleksei pass my bloodied figure as I join the line on the east side of the sanctuary. Rafael, Hugo, Luca, and Jonah stand quietly, sparing brief glances of commiseration before focusing on the dismemberment of the man I just killed.

He's not the first, and he won't be the last.

But I look forward to the day when the decision of whom to kill is mine, not Conrad's, because there are several names on my list.

At the very top?

The reason I'm stuck at Blackchapel Manor participating in fucked-up lessons.

Louis Petit, my bastard father.

CHAPTER ONE

ALLISON FIELDS

PRESENT DAY

The romantic melody of *La Vie en Rose* swells to life on the TV screen as *Sabrina* continues playing in the background. The 1954 version with Audrey Hepburn and Humphrey Bogart is one of my favorite films, and it only seems right that it provides the soundtrack for packing my suitcase to Paris.

"*Hold me close and hold me fast...*," I sing softly, leaving my room to grab scissors from the office to open the plastic covering on my new outlet converter. When I return, the song has faded to allow Sabrina to narrate the start of the movie.

The glamorous life of the wealthy family that employs her father. Her longing for the family's youngest son, David.

It's a modern fairytale in the making, and my hand stills as a familiar wave of sadness seeps around the excitement for my trip.

For all my foolish hopes growing up. For all the escapes romantic stories provided. I never imagined myself as the kind of girl who got a *happily ever after*.

My life perpetually exists in the *before*.

Dramatic childhood. Tragic loneliness. The necessary backstory *before* the heroine meets her prince and she blooms from a tough little seed into a beautiful rose—into a woman whose *after* is full of love and joy.

Humming absentmindedly, I lift my shirt as if in a trance, musical notes spinning a gossamer web of whimsical optimism and somber reality. Romantic fiction contrasting with my life.

The sharp tip of the scissors gently presses into my stomach, and I sigh at the sight of cool metal creating a dip in my belly. With a little more pressure, they'll puncture the skin.

If I go far enough, it'll probably pierce a vital organ.

I could bleed out.

Too slow and too painful.

Shaking off the moment of morbid curiosity, I drop the scissors on my nightstand after snipping off a corner of the packaging.

It'll be my first time out of the country tomorrow, and despite its work purpose, I'm excited for the short reprieve from home. Like Sabrina, I yearn for a change in circumstances.

Unlike her, I doubt I'll receive one.

A perfunctory knock on the bedroom door startles me from my thoughts before my roommate enters without waiting for a response. Her two rambunctious dogs race inside and bump excitedly into my bed, causing the stack of folded clothes in my suitcase to topple, and I bite my tongue from lashing out.

It's not their fault their owner keeps them cooped up inside the apartment rather than letting them expend their energy at the complex's dog park. That she doesn't curb their wild behavior. That their high energy sends my pulse racing, desperate to find calm again.

"Where's your charging cord?" Bailey rummages through the odds and ends scattered on the shelving along the wall without so much as a 'hello' or 'sorry for barging in.'

"Why? What happened to yours?" I ask as I right the fallen tower of clothing and connect the thin, restraining bands across the stack to prevent it from tumbling again.

"The stupid thing stopped working. Found it!" She pulls a neatly wrapped cord from a box half-hidden underneath a pile of papers. "It's not like you need this anyway. The box comes with two."

My tongue aches from the increased pressure of my teeth to avoid starting an argument.

Like I always do these days.

Bailey and I used to be good friends. We met freshman year of college and stuck together through tough exams and bitter breakups—hers, not mine. That's why we chose to live as roommates after graduation.

But that was five years ago, and a lot has changed. Namely, she quit her job two years ago, making me the sole provider in our apartment. The only one standing between us and homelessness or starvation.

The plastic package finally pops open but slices the side of my finger with burning precision. I hiss in pain as blood wells from the one inch cut, immediately grabbing a tissue and pressing it to the wound.

Bailey doesn't bother to check on me. Or thank me for letting her borrow the cord. She saunters out of the room with Roscoe and Palmer trailing behind, leaving my door open to let in her cat next.

"Hey, Pretty Kitty," I murmur, sinking onto the edge of the bed. The black cat meows in greeting.

Living this way with Bailey—a ghost until she needs something from me, burdened with keeping us afloat—has made me into a shell of the person I used to be.

Not that I've ever truly been free of being the responsible one. The defense between a world of trouble and those I care about. Before it was my family, and now it's Bailey.

Sometimes I wonder what she'd do without me. What everyone would do if I were gone.

But there lies the rub. Why I have these urges to put an end to my misery and why I never will.

I hate pain.

I could never truly harm myself.

And my life isn't all bad. I'm going to Paris. My first international trip. I've got things to live for.

Or the hope that there will be more to live for, eventually, since everything will be the same once I return home.

After turning up the volume in the hopes that the movie will drown out my pessimistic thoughts, I peel off the stained tissue, see I've stopped bleeding, and resume packing.

Maybe the City of Lights will change my life.

And maybe that's just another fairytale that won't come true.

CHAPTER TWO

MATHIAS

"*Dites-leur de nous envoyer les contrats signés avant la fin des activités, sinon l'accord est annulé.*" The command barely leaves my lips before I end the phone call with my lawyers. Petit Enterprises's attempts to fuck me over cement my decision to rip the company to shreds once it's under my ownership.

Of course, that was always the plan, but now I'm even more determined to see it through.

CEO Louis Petit is a narcissistic asshole who has left leather-heeled imprints across Europe in his quest to dominate the legal and blackmarket trade of pharmaceuticals.

He's also my father.

"*Qu'allez-vous faire s'ils ne se conforment pas?*" Luca asks. We've been best friends for over twenty years, ever since we arrived at Blackchapel Manor as two angry youths itching to break free from our tethers. So, he knows how much is riding on this deal.

I answer in French as we navigate through the building lobby. "Nothing. Because they'll sign the contracts. There's no other option for Petit with creditors breathing down his neck—specifically the *Cosa Nostra*. Unless he wants to take a permanent dive into the Seine, he'll stop fucking around and agree to the deal. It means a massive payout for him and The Syndicate."

Not that Petit will truly get to enjoy the influx of cash. He'll be dead long before then, but not by the Sicilian mob.

By me.

The bastard son he abandoned.

Hugo's father, Conrad Steele, raised us at Blackchapel Manor. Trained us in the art of murder and manipulation to one day bring down The Syndicate, an underground network that controls the blackmarket and facets of world governments. The majority of The Syndicate's leaders also happen to be our fathers.

Conrad had once been part of the organization before they blackballed him. We never learned the reason why he was ousted; only that he sought revenge through the sons of its leaders.

Unfortunately for him, none of us took kindly to being raised as mercenaries from such tender ages—stolen from our mothers in some cases—which is why we refused to give him the satisfaction of seeing his life's work come to fruition.

He died a bitter old man.

A small consolation prize for the torture we endured.

Luca and I step outside where a gray blanket of rain covers Paris. Hiking up the collar of my longcoat, I imagine the café crème and warm almond croissant awaiting me in the town car parked on the street. Those two items are always available when I visit my father's country or else it'd be someone's head.

At least that's what my employees fear.

To be fair, I've never decapitated a man for forgetting my mid-morning pick-me-up, though I suppose there's a first time for everything.

"I'm over these games," Luca grumbles from beside me, a grimace painting his tan face. "When we return home, I'm—"

Squealing tires pierce the air as a white van whips around the corner. A flurry of car horns erupts at the haphazard driving, but it's the sliding open of the side door that draws my attention. A masked man hangs onto a handle above the opening while his other arm holds an automatic rifle—its barrel pointed straight at me.

Bullets explode from the weapon in one continuous sweep as the van speeds by, but before I have time to take cover, something slams into my side, dragging me down to the sidewalk as car windows shatter from above.

Screams and sirens form a distant bubble. Like my ears are stuffed with cotton, muffling the sounds. Raindrops sting my eyes as I stare up at the sky, and I lick away the wetness seeping between my lips.

Despite the ice running through my veins—from being targeted and the February chill—warmth envelops my limbs. Warmth that's emanating from whoever pushed me out of harm's way and now lays motionless over my body.

"*Êtes-vous d'accord?*"

No answer.

"*Es-tu blessé?*"

Still nothing.

Rolling over, I switch positions with my savior, so I'm hovering over them.

Her.

It's a woman.

Frizzy brown curls cling to the concrete and her eyes remain closed behind rain-splattered glasses. Dark patches of blood spread beneath the fabric of her pink sweater and unzipped raincoat—one blooming on her bicep and the other on her thigh.

This woman—*this stranger*—intercepted at least two bullets that were meant for me.

Why?

"Mathias, are you okay?" Luca army crawls across the pavement, a cut above his eyebrow leaving a trail of blood down his cheek and neck. "Who the fuck was that?"

"I don't know, but I intend to find out." As the Blackchapel Bastards, me, Luca, and our five brothers-in-arms, have no shortage of enemies. It could be any number of organizations looking to kill one or all of us. Hell, it could be Louis fucking Petit if he caught wind of my true intentions for him and his company.

He knows I'm his son, and he's aware of Conrad's desire for revenge. But I'm unsure if he knows that desire didn't die with Conrad.

It still lives within me.

"First, we need to get her to the hospital before she bleeds out."

"An ambulance is on its way. Let them handle it. We need to leave."

"No!" I bark, and stunned confusion passes over Luca's face.

I'm the calm one.

Nothing affects my poise.

Except, apparently, a mystery woman diving in front of bullets meant for me.

Attempting to defuse the raging storm inside, I take a breath before continuing in a forced tone of calm. "No, she threw herself into a barrage of bullets for me, and I want to know why. I'm going to the hospital to ensure she survives."

Luca remains silent before sighing. "Fine. Do you want me to go with you as backup in case those assholes try to finish the job?"

"I can handle myself. Go back to the hotel and notify everyone about the situation." My brain buzzes with questions about this woman's motives, but a sliver of my usual cool, analytical self emerges long enough to give instructions. "Start pulling footage from the traffic lights to see if we can track the vehicle and find the culprits. Get Jonah to handle the security cameras from this building."

"I'm on it. Be careful."

An ambulance and several police cars roar to a stop on the street as Luca slips into the crowd—dodging curious onlookers—when a moan of pain comes from my rescuer. Her eyes blink open to reveal blurry blue irises behind her glasses, so I carefully remove the frames and slide them into my coat pocket to improve my view.

Eyes are the windows to the soul.

These windows better offer damn quick revelations, because I hate being kept in the dark.

"What... I need—" She tries to sit up then winces, falling back to the concrete.

"Don't move," I command in English. It seems my mystery woman is American with her blunt consonants and hard vowels. "You've been shot and need to remain still."

Instinctively, my hands had moved to put pressure on her wounds, but they aren't doing much to stem the tide of blood, the viscous fluid pulsing from beneath my palms.

Two paramedics arrive with a gurney and immediately take over. Starting an IV. Pressing gauze into the injuries. And within five minutes we're loaded into the ambulance speeding towards the hospital.

The uniformed men work on the woman as I contemplate her small, curvy form and casually confiscate her purse. Searching for clues as to who she is. What she wants.

Receipts for fast food. A few Euros. A North Carolina driver's license registered to Allison Fields.

My jaw clenches at the discovery of her identity. It's the first solid bit of information concerning today's events I've gotten, and Rafe can use it to figure out Miss Fields's secrets.

No one does what she did without a reason. There's always an angle. A price to pay.

And I need to know hers.

CHAPTER THREE

ALLISON

Repetitive beeping tickles the edge of my consciousness. *What is that? Someone's alarm?* I fight to focus enough to decipher its source, but a cloud of fuzziness obscures the sound.

I should turn it off.

It's probably annoying Bailey.

A whimper of fear lodges in my throat when my arm refuses to move, and my leg lies anchored to the bed like leadened weight.

Did I sleep wrong? Cut off the blood supply to my limbs? Will I be able to walk around Paris?

Wait... Paris.

Rainy, cold.

My coworkers wanted coffee after a morning of meetings.

I'd gasp if I was fully awake. Instead, I'm stuck hovering between sleep and wakefulness as the memory of the crazy van and shooter plays like a high-octane movie in my head. There was a man. He stood in the line of fire. And, *oh my god*, I jumped in front of a bullet.

The roar of my pounding heart fills my ears. *What was I thinking?* I'm not an action hero. Or indestructible. Or a person who seeks out pain.

I avoid it at all costs.

To my own detriment.

Swallowing past the anxious lump in my throat, I swim through the brain fog and open my eyes to an unfamiliar room potent with that metallic smell of sterile medical supplies.

Blurry shapes surround me. The blinds are closed. No lights except for colorful beams from the medical monitors. Neon green. Bright flashing red.

Machines, not people.

I thought my coworkers might be here, but I'm alone. *Always alone.*

Tears form a hazy film over my vision. I shouldn't be shocked by their absence. We're friendly, but we don't hang out together after work. We go on to live our separate lives. So, why would they show up at my hospital room?

And maybe they don't know what happened. They were inside the café when everything went down.

The possibility offers a modicum of comfort when something shifts in my periphery. I tilt my head to the side, straining to figure out if it was real or imaginary.

There's more rustling.

I'm not alone.

Someone sits in the chair next to me, but the back is pushed against the wall, leaving the stranger wrapped in shadows. No wonder I missed them on my first pass around the room.

"Hello," I croak, desperate for a drink of water to get rid of this scratchy feeling in my mouth.

"You're awake." His gravelly voice erects warning signs in my head. *Why is there a man in my room? Was he watching me sleep?* A passing conversation floats in from the hallway, and that's when I realize he spoke English instead of French.

"A-Are... you... a doctor?" Each word scrapes against my raw vocal cords. It's a miracle I can even speak with nerves threatening to clog my throat.

"You don't recognize the man you rescued?"

My fingers dig into the thin blanket covering my lap as a chill works its way down my spine. Perhaps his presence shouldn't make me wary, but if he was the intended target of those shooters, then I can only imagine what kind of trouble he's in to warrant an assassination attempt.

And now he's in my room.

He was waiting for me to wake up. But for what purpose? Because I don't get the impression he's overcome by gratitude.

"No... S-Sorry... I'm glad you're okay, though."

"Thanks to you." He remains in the shadows, so I can't see his face. Maybe there's a reason he's hiding. Maybe it's one of those scenarios where if I can identify him, then he'll have to kill me. *Unless he already thinks you can identify him after saving him from a drive-by...*

Fear spikes in my blood at what that could mean for me, and the numbers jump on the screen monitoring my pulse.

"Where am I?" I ask, frantic for information. I need to let someone know where I am. I need to not be alone. *Alway alone.*

Silence hangs in the air before he grunts in displeasure.

"St. Martin's Hospital. You had emergency surgery to remove a bullet. One grazed your arm, but the other landed in your thigh. According to the doctors, you were extremely lucky in the placement. They managed to avoid hitting any major nerves or arteries."

"That's a relief." My shaky attempt at a smile fails miserably. "Did the doctors mention how long I have to stay here?"

"For a few days. Until you're safe from infection," he drawls.

Another pregnant pause falls over us, punctuated by the constant beeping that woke me earlier. It's unnerving—a foghorn in misty waters warning of danger.

"Why are you here?" *Please don't say to tie up loose ends. To kill me for getting involved in some sort of street war.* All of those true crime documentaries I've watched come back to bite me in the ass as the dangerous possibilities pile high and skyrocket my anxiety with it.

"That's the crux of it, isn't it?" He finally stands and steps forward, a shadowy behemoth rising from the underworld like Hades himself. Bracing one hand on the hospital bed, his large body dominates the small space, and I gasp at his size. "We're strangers. Or, at least, I have no idea who *you* are."

"I-I don't know you either."

"Yet you threw yourself on top of me. Blocked the spray of bullets headed my way. A brave thing to do for a mere *stranger*," he stresses the word again, the white of his teeth snarling from the shadows.

"I wasn't thinking about that."

I acted on instinct—a stupid one, too, not courageous. Most people might pat themselves on the back for being brave or heroic. Might be proud to know that when push comes to shove, they do the right thing; they run toward danger if it means saving a life.

But I don't feel pride in my actions. I don't feel brave. I feel sick to my stomach.

A low chuckle rumbles from his chest, but it's far from amused. It's the ominous roar before a tiger pounces.

"You didn't think becoming my savior might ingratiate yourself to me? Might make me lower my guard enough for you to steal whatever you're after?"

"No! I have no idea what you're talking about." There's an obvious plea in my voice as that song from *Wicked* plays in my mind.

No good deed goes unpunished.

But what will my punishment be?

"You're going to play innocent?" he scoffs, a sneer twisting his lips.

"I'm not playing at anything. Please, you have to believe me. All I know is I saw the gun, I saw you, and my body reacted. There wasn't much thinking going on at all."

His fingers tighten on the blanket near my hips, strapping me to the bed like a cocooned butterfly. *Or a spider's doomed prey.*

"So, you lack the universal instinct of self-preservation?" Disbelief tinges his voice as he lowers his head to mine. This close the silver sparks in his eyes blend to onyx, and my breath freezes at the hostile suspicion.

"Apparently," I whisper. A coughing fit bursts free, and I use it as an opportunity to hide, turning my face away from his.

He has no idea the suicidal thoughts I've dealt with in the past. How sometimes I wonder if death would be better than the life I'm currently living. One that's full of stress and trouble.

Did that subconsciously control my actions?

Was saving him some twisted way of ending my misery?

Only you could twist a selfless act into one of unconscious selfishness.

The man retreats long enough to pour water into a plastic cup. He lowers it to my mouth but doesn't allow me to take control of it. Instead, he directs the straw between my lips, waits a few seconds, then pulls it out, quietly deciding when I've had enough.

It's high-handed, but the only emotion I can muster is gratitude as the water soothes my dry mouth and throat.

"You were willing to trade your life for mine." He places the cup on the tray by my bed. "For no other reason than the kindness of your heart. Danger strikes, and instead of running away from it, your body tells you to run towards it."

"I guess so," I say wearily. I'm not going to voice the other possibility: that I subconsciously did it on purpose.

I don't think he'd believe me anyway.

Fatigue weighs on my eyelids. All I really want is to fade back into sleep where I don't have to worry about thoughts of hurting myself, and I don't have to deal with this man who may or may not want me dead. Or silenced. Or whatever else men who get shot at and have distrust radiating from them in waves want.

"We'll see if that's true or not, won't we?" He studies my inert form in one long sweep, as if willing my secrets to reveal themselves under his powerful gaze, before he turns on his heel and heads for the door.

"Wait!" *What are you doing? Let him go!* But my messed-up brain has other ideas, curiosity and dread refusing to let go until I know one thing.

He pauses but keeps his back to me.

"Who are you?"

"If you're as innocent as you say, it's best you don't know, *mon ange.*"

Then he's gone, and I'm left to spiral over what the hell just happened.

CHAPTER FOUR

MATHIAS

"Where are we on finding those motherfuckers?" I strip off my blood-splattered suit and toss it onto the hotel carpet. I need a shower, a drink, and something to focus on other than Allison Fields.

She was nervous during questioning, but I hadn't detected any lies. Which means she's more of a mystery now than she was before we spoke.

I'm starting to think that her jumping in front of those bullets was a random act of kindness—a thoughtless act with no regard for her safety.

Who cares?

I don't have time for a woman. No matter how intriguing she may be.

I've got actual problems to deal with rather than puzzling over her rash decisions. Or wondering why no one else showed up at the hospital looking for her. Or remembering how thirsty she'd been as I held her cup and worrying if a nurse would refill it for her soon.

A couple of buttons pop off my shirt as it rips open from my agitated movements. *Dammit.* Now, she has me ruining my clothes like some clumsy beast rather than the controlled man I am.

Luca leans against the doorjamb, an indecipherable expression on his face. "Rafe tracked the van's license plate to a shell corporation owned by Enzo D'Amora. So, the good news is the drive-by wasn't meant for you. It was dear old Dad trying to kill me instead."

"What the hell? I thought he wanted to bring you into the family business."

Enzo D'Amora is the head of Boston's Italian mafia, and despite abandoning Luca at Blackchapel Manor, the don has made several overtures to his bastard son, inviting him into the D'Amora fold. Because if there's one thing the Italian mafia loves more than wielding power, it's blood ties.

Out of all of our fathers, Enzo was the closest to Conrad. He may have gone along with The Syndicate's decision to blackball Conrad, but he'd trusted the man enough to leave Luca with him after his mother died.

Sometimes I wonder if Enzo regretted that choice, since his friend's bitterness toward The Syndicate became more obvious over the years.

Like Enzo's trying to make up for years of neglect by welcoming Luca back into the family fold.

"Maybe he changed his mind after I attended his birthday celebration. Perhaps the fallout of associating with an illegitimate son is too much for his old heart to weather." Luca shrugs, as if learning his father ordered a hit on him is an everyday occurrence.

"Let's set up extra surveillance on D'Amora in case he plans to send someone else to finish the job."

"Jonah's on it already. He and Dmitri have a Blackthorn team heading there now. Oh, and the jet is ready when you are. I called ahead to move up our departure."

"Good thinking. Let them know I want wheels up in thirty." That'll give me enough time for a quick shower and to pack my carry-on. Then I can relax for six hours.

And absolutely not dwell on the woman I'm leaving behind.

***

Once our private jet lands in Boston, I text everyone to meet me in the main living room of the manor. What used to be a twisted sort of home school for us has become our base and shelter.

A vast improvement because Conrad Steele is gone.

"Rafe, I need you to run a background check on Allison Fields."

"The woman who risked her life for you?" he asks from his spot on the couch playing a racing game on the huge TV mounted on the wall.

"Yeah, and I want to know why. Even if the attack was meant for Luca, it's still suspicious how she leaped in front of me. Maybe it's a distraction from another trap lying in wait."

"Always so paranoid."

"For good reason." I smack the back of Rafe's head. As the youngest of our brotherhood, he gets the little brother treatment. "We're the Blackchapel Bastards. They don't call us that because we're fucking choir boys. We have enemies, and the only way to stay alive is by remaining multiple steps ahead of them."

"Yeah, yeah, yeah." Rafe groans, keeping his focus on the screen where a red car flies past his black one. He's heard this spiel before. They all have. But I'll repeat it until I'm blue in the face if it means keeping my family safe.

"Has anyone heard from Alek today?" I ask, changing the subject to our brother currently locked in prison.

He's been undercover the past eighteen months to infiltrate his and Dmitri's father's organization.

Sergei Petrov is the world's premier arms dealer and a dangerous son of a bitch. He's aware of Dmitri's existence, but their mother escaped Sergei's hold before he learned of Aleksei. We're hoping that secret pays off by having Alek climb the ladder of men leading straight to Sergei's place on top.

The rest of us don't have that advantage with our fathers. They're well aware of our identities, and while a few are curious about bringing an illegitimate son into their business, the majority remain ambivalent, focused on what matters to them: money and power.

Like my dad, Louis Petit.

Too bad he'll be losing both things soon enough.

"I called him this morning," Dmitri says. "Oleg Kasik approached him at dinner last night. With Alek's release in three months, they're planning on taking him to Petrov where he'll learn his next mission. It's a good sign. Means he's gained Sergei's trust enough to see the inner workings of the compound. That'll help when it's time to burn it to the fucking ground."

We all nod, looking forward to the day when the game of revenge we've been playing since boyhood finally comes to an end.

CHAPTER FIVE

ALLISON

"Have you seen my glasses?" The hospital is finally releasing me, so I can fly home later this afternoon, but I really don't want to travel blind as a bat. I gently shake the bedding again and pray the glasses appear.

"Nope... Maybe you lost them at the scene," Jenna, a fellow coworker, says.

Frowning, I finish dressing in the clean clothes she brought and consider the possibility.

That day is a fuzzy memory. The only thing I remember with painful clarity is the mysterious man who appeared in my hospital room afterward.

Large. Imposing. Attractive in a villainous way. I shake that particular observation off. Romanticizing bad men belongs in books and movies, not my real life.

"Maybe I can get a prescription for a new pair before we leave." Otherwise, I'll be relying on acquaintances to safely fly me from Paris to Raleigh.

They're capable, but it'd be uncomfortable and awkward as hell.

"Let me ask a nurse," she says, heading toward the door. "I don't want to be responsible if you cross the street during a red light and get nailed by a Vespa."

I hide an unsurprised grimace by pulling on a hoodie.

Do I want to be reliant on other people? No, life has taught me that independence is best.

But would it be nice if I could count on those around me?

Damn straight.

"She said you'll have to see an optometrist for the glasses." Jenna huffs as she strolls back into the room. "Looks like I'm your new chauffeur until you get home. You have spares there, right?"

"Yeah, I'll be fine." And I'm determined to not be a burden to Jenna. She doesn't deserve being my babysitter just because I'm cursed with bad eyesight.

Geez, I'm a wreck. Practically blind, arm in a sling, and forced to be wheeled around due to my injured leg.

It'll be a miracle if I get home without adding to my menagerie of ailments.

***

"Mom? Dad? I'm here!" No one answers my greeting as the front door slams behind me, though my brother Josh is on the couch watching an anime show.

"Where is everyone?" I ask, using my crutches to hobble into the living room. Driving for two and a half hours wasn't the best thing for my sore leg. Tensing and relaxing the healing muscles with each press on the gas and brake sucked. But after almost dying in Paris two weeks ago, I felt nostalgic for home, so I let my family know I was visiting for the weekend.

Stupid, really.

When have my parents ever comforted me? Since when have they had the emotional capacity to deal with anything I might be struggling with?

That's why I still haven't shared about the bullet wounds that sent me to the hospital. I figured I'd make up a random excuse for my injuries.

Who doesn't share the truth with their family?

People who know it'd result in more work to calm and reassure rather than a soothing embrace.

"Don't know," Josh mutters. "I haven't seen them."

Disappointment dampens my spirits, and my gaze trails toward my car parked outside, tempted to drive back home despite the long journey I just completed.

How quickly I'm reminded that those fantasies of *maybe this time will be different, maybe this time they'll care* are puffs of smoke.

Here and gone within a breath.

Joining Josh on the couch, I prop my feet on the scuffed footrest and watch as two characters skateboard down a mountain until the screen flicks to black.

"You don't have to turn it off," I say as Josh tosses the remote to the cushion beside me. "Where are you going?"

He mumbles a short sentence I don't quite catch.

"What?"

With his back turned to me, another garbled response hangs in the air, but this time I let it go. If I ask a third time, he'll accuse me of not listening and get pissed. It's happened before.

His footsteps fade the further he gets from the living room, and the prick of tears behind my eyes has me rapidly blinking up at the popcorn ceiling.

Don't cry.

Don't cry.

So what if I drove over a hundred miles just to be ignored and abandoned? It's not personal. It's their problem, not mine.

I repeat things my therapist has said—facts I logically know are true—but emotionally?

They don't do much to ease the pain of feeling unwanted.

And always being alone.

CHAPTER SIX

ALLISON

One million dollars.

That can't be right.

Curiosity creeps through the numbness that's cocooned me since returning from Paris and that disastrous weekend at my parents'. I tap around the banking app trying to figure out what's going on.

Someone hijacked my account. It's the only explanation.

But who?

And why?

Hackers steal money. They don't deposit a boatload of it.

So why is my account—one previously depleted by groceries and bills—suddenly flush with a million dollars?

The bank didn't even call to question whether or not I was some kind of drug mule with that amount of cash. I only discovered the deposit when their weekly balance text appeared on my phone.

Aren't large deposits supposed to be questionable?

I scroll to the transaction, hit the little arrow to expand the details, and scan the screen. One million dollars from Blackchapel Incorporated.

Who the hell is that?

A quick internet search later, and I'm clicking through the company's website. A list of board members appears, along with a picture of two extremely attractive men posed in front of a Blackchapel sign.

The man on the left immediately draws my attention. I didn't get a well-lit view of the guy I saved, but there's no mistaking those stormy eyes and intense aura.

Mathias Beaumont—Blackchapel Incorporated's CEO.

More of the ever-present numbness chips away.

It's been three weeks since being discharged from the hospital. Twenty-one days since I flew home.

When I didn't hear from him again, I'd hoped that meant I was out of the woods. That he believed me when I said I didn't have an ulterior motive for saving him. That whatever trouble he was mixed up in didn't involve me.

But now there's this—one million dollars.

Like it's some kind of recompense for saving his life.

Maybe it is.

The transaction looks legitimate, and based on my fifteen minutes on this website, he certainly has the money to spare. Blackchapel Inc. is an internationally renowned billion dollar company.

Perhaps this is Mathias's way of making us square. Of subtly letting me know that our connection is severed. That there won't be repercussions for inserting myself into his dangerous life.

Bailey's cat slinks between my legs with a plaintive meow. No help at all. "Not now, Pretty Kitty. I'm in the middle of a minor freak out."

I don't plan on blowing a million dollars in the next month, but what if I relieve part of the burden on my shoulders by paying off my student loans, and then it comes out that there was a mistake, and Mathias wants the money back?

I don't have twenty grand lying around. That's why I still have the freaking loans.

You can try calling him. There's a number listed on the site below the address of the company headquarters. It probably goes straight to a receptionist who has never even met her boss's boss's boss.

Maybe if I leave a paper trail confirming the deposit's veracity...

Even if he doesn't respond, it'll prove that I tried to fix the error but was ignored, taking the blame off me if anything goes awry in the future.

As the best plan I can come up with, I draft an email to the corporate address listed, along with a personal one to Mathias. First initial, last name, at *blackchapelinc.com* seems to be their email formula.

Fingers crossed he receives a copy of the message.

With that done, I immediately head over to the student loan site and pay off the $20,000 before chickening out. A *thank you* confirmation appears on the screen.

And just like that, I'm debt-free.

Excitement fights for supremacy—a million dollars can do a lot for a person. But any emotion lately has been hard to hold on to.

Waking up in that Parisian hospital alone, save Mathias. Receiving a cold welcome on my visit home. Dealing with Bailey's unchanging attitude. It's what I feared would happen before the trip, which is nothing.

Nothing's changed.

Nothing will ever change.

Numbness weaves around me again to dull the sensation of everything else when the front door bangs against the entry wall before slamming shut.

Bailey's home.

Tucking my phone in my pocket, I walk out to the living room with Pretty Kitty hot on my heels, still whining for food because she's always a starving little gremlin. A cat and two dogs—Bailey's trio of pets that have also fallen under my care.

"Bad day at work?" It's a loose term for Bailey's current delivery driver position since she barely puts in the effort to earn much from the gig. For the amount of time she works each week, it's better classified as a hobby versus a part-time job.

"It's always a bad day." She stomps around the kitchen like an angry rhino before grabbing one of my Gatorades from the fridge.

I don't bother calling her on it because it would start a fight. One she's itching to have with her obvious attitude.

Sighing, I rub a hand over the tightness in my chest. Every day is a fight with her, and it wears on my psyche. *Wore* on my psyche.

These days I feel like I've finally broken.

Bailey. My family. They finally won.

But my current situation could soon be a distant memory. Because I have enough money to get out. Disappear from all of this.

You don't have to stay here. A voice sing-songs in my brain. *You don't have to live this way.*

Then a whisper of defiance.

Rally one more time.

CHAPTER SEVEN

MATHIAS

To: Mathias Beaumont; Blackchapel Incorporated
From: Allison Fields
Subject: A Banking Error?
To Whom It May Concern:
I'm investigating the unexpected deposit of a large sum of money into my private checking account. The transaction went through sometime last night. I'm attaching a screenshot for reference.
Please let me know how we can rectify this situation.
Thank you!
Allison Fields

***

The surprise message from Allison steals my focus from the man indicating where I should sign to complete the Petit deal. She's questioning the validity of one million dollars in her bank account?

I suppose it's smart, but most people wouldn't balk at such a windfall. They'd accept fate—whether from an error or not—and go on their merry way, but not my confounding guardian angel.

"One more signature here, sir." Another document slides in front of me, and I scratch my name across the bottom, right next to Louis Petit's flamboyant penmanship. Big swoops and exaggerated lines.

He hasn't spoken much during this final meeting between our business attorneys to close the deal, but that isn't to say he hasn't gotten his message across. Muted glares and annoyed huffs have wafted across the long conference table the past forty-five minutes.

He's pissed.

Losing one's company due to outmaneuvering will do that to a person. Even if it does come with a sizable purchase price.

I type a quick message to the woman who checks Blackchapel Inc.'s corporate email account, telling her to ignore Allison's message because I'll deal with it personally, before opening a new email draft.

***

To: *Allison Fields*
From: *Mathias Beaumont*
Subject: *RE: A Banking Error?*
There wasn't an error. The deposit is legal and final.
Mathias Beaumont
CEO of Blackchapel Incorporated

***

After weeks of working to uncover D'Amora's motive for wanting Luca dead and closing the Petit deal, you'd think my time would be fully occupied, yet my thoughts continued to drift to Allison.

Especially after responding to her email and receiving nothing in return.

Except for the knowledge that she still hasn't spent the money I put in her bank account as payment for saving my life.

I don't like being indebted to people, and a life debt? That's untenable. A million dollars should be enough to make us even.

That's what I told myself, anyway, but it's hardly doing its job while sitting untouched in her account.

Every day I check it, and every day it's the same.

She withdrew a minuscule $19,678 the first day, which went straight to the government for her student loans, but that's it.

She could do anything with the money. Go on another trip, buy a house, get a new car. *Anything*. The world is her oyster. Yet she's done nothing, opting instead to use money earned from her job to pay for things.

And I don't fucking understand—an uncomfortable sensation that's become something of a habit with the woman.

"Back to checking your girl's bank account?" Luca asks as he enters the great room with a towel draped over his shoulder. He must be on his way to swim laps in the manor's indoor pool—his preferred way to relax because of the quiet underwater.

"I don't know what you're talking about." I slam the laptop shut.

Luca chuckles. "You realize we're capable of tracking each other's movements, right? So we know you sent Allison a fuckton of cash she's leaving unused, and we know that you're monitoring her not using it. Why don't you just go see her if you're that obsessed?"

"I'm not obsessed." I've always had a penchant for puzzles, and Allison is a five-thousand piece Rembrandt I'm determined to solve. "Don't be ridiculous. She's an enigma. I'm trying to figure out how she fits into the drive-by."

Liar.

Luca calls me on it.

"I thought we agreed she was a random civilian who got caught up in the moment, and you're lucky for it. You really think this girl—a former straight-A student, perfect attendance, no speeding tickets to her name—is part of a larger scheme to either swindle or kill you?"

No, but I'm not admitting that aloud. It'll confirm his false belief of my obsession with Allison.

I don't like loose ends, and that's what she feels like because she doesn't react normally to anything. Rather, she doesn't react how I believe a regular person, not raised in an assassin's manor, would behave.

Stretching to my full height, I tuck the laptop under my arm and walk towards the door, a vague plan beginning to form. Perhaps it's time I gather intel up close and personal since distance has my mind spinning in circles.

"Have fun in Raleigh." Luca smirks, and I flip him the bird because he's right about my destination.

A text to our pilot lets him know to fuel the jet for a short trip. The plan is to touch down in North Carolina in two hours.

I'm going to figure out what the hell is going on with my mystery woman and finally lay this fixation to rest.

CHAPTER EIGHT

MATHIAS

The town car parks in front of a dingy apartment building after picking me up at the private airfield. Beige paint tries to make the structure blend into the woods surrounding it, but all the color does is scream the seventies.

A fortune in Allison's account yet she chooses to live here.

It boggles the mind.

"I won't be long," I tell the driver before exiting the car. It's warmer here than it is in Boston, but there's enough of a chill to warrant my coat.

Recalling her apartment number, 19H, I take the stairs two at a time. They creak beneath my weight, and the only positive thing going for them is that they're covered, because if left open to the elements, they'd rot in no time.

Finding the chipped black door heralding Allison's address, I knock next to the peephole and wait. A teal welcome mat crunches beneath my shoes as I shift backwards to read the cheerful cursive. *Hello, Gorgeous!* The peppy greeting and bright burst of color is incongruous with an otherwise drab environment.

Shuffling occurs behind the door along with a chorus of barks and growls.

So she has dogs.

The door creaks open an inch, and then another, as I watch a sliver of Allison beat back the canines rushing the entry. The dogs refuse to listen to her commands, forcing her to squeeze through the cracked opening to step outside and shut the door on their rabid excitement.

It's obvious she didn't check the peephole before answering, because when she finally turns my way, her eyes widen, her mouth dropping open in shock.

My comment about her lack of self-preservation pops to mind again, and my teeth will soon be dust at the rate she has me grinding them together in frustration.

The wise thing to do when you have a visitor is check the damn peephole because anyone could be on the other side of the door. I could have shot her dead in two seconds flat the moment the door opened. I could have barged inside her apartment with one forceful shove.

"M... Mathias?"

A sense of satisfaction dissipates some of the annoyance roiling through me. She remembers my name. It's evidence of the only logical thing she's done so far—research who gifted her a mountain of cash.

"Let's take a walk." I skip the niceties. A habit to get straight to the point rather than wasting time by bullshitting about nothing.

My hand automatically reaches for hers to tug her downstairs away from the barking dogs who are still making a racket.

The wound in her thigh doesn't seem to pain her. No limping or wincing with each step.

"Your injuries don't bother you?" I ask against my better judgment. The state of her health isn't why I flew hundreds of miles; the mystery of her refusal to spend my money is. I've come to figure out the puzzle that is Allison Marie Fields, and that doesn't include monitoring her healing progress.

"There's some residual pain, but overall, it's like it never happened. Except for the scars."

My clasp tightens around her fingers. Scars are a consequence of life. I've certainly got my fair share after years of lessons and punishments from Conrad.

So why the fuck does the thought of Allison's soft curves marred by scars make me want to find D'Amora's men and slit their throats?

Because you've been raised with a steady thirst for revenge, I rationalize, determined to maintain my composure.

They'll get what's coming to them soon enough from Luca, and that should be enough to appease the hunger for their blood.

But they left marks on Allison.

My w—

I slam the door on that train of thought. She's not *my* anything. She's just a puzzle.

Aware that nosy neighbors could eavesdrop on our conversation, I guide her between two trees for privacy. A thousand questions are on the tip of my tongue, but I go with the most relevant one first.

"Why do you live here?"

"Excuse me?" She pulls her hand away, and I wonder if my grip accidently hurt her since it's the same arm where she was shot. Did I tug too hard and irritate the muscle? Kick up that *residual pain*?

"Why do you live in this shithole when you could move somewhere better? Safer?"

"This is a safe area, and I live here because I signed a lease." Allison crosses her arms over her chest, and automatically, my gaze falls to the generous swell of her breasts beneath the thin shirt. The way they easily shape to their new position lets me know she's not wearing a bra, and I grit my teeth at the realization.

Why the fuck is she opening her door to strangers without being properly dressed?

"Why are you here?" She retreats another step. As if she has a chance of outrunning me if she tried. "How did you find me?"

"I put a million dollars in your bank account. You think it wasn't easy to find your address, too?"

"Touché." A flash of understanding tightens her features, then her eyebrows lift in worry. "Is this about the money? Please tell me it wasn't a mistake, or if it was, that you don't need it paid back immediately. I have the majority of it, but I used some to pay my student loans. I emailed you about it in case it was a mistake. You said it was *legal and final.*"

"It wasn't a mistake." I stuff my hands in my coat pockets to avoid the temptation to shake sense into the woman.

She's like a fluffy little bunny flinching at every noise in the forest, except for the ones that actually herald danger. *Bullets from a drive-by. A stranger knocking on her door.* None of that fazes her, but a substantial addition to her bank account with an official email of approval from the CEO of a billion dollar company? *That's* what gets her hackles up.

"The only mistake being made is your stubborn refusal to spend more of it. You could have bought a house and moved away from this place."

"Why does it matter if I don't spend your money?" Her eyes crinkle at the corners as her mind works to understand. Square lenses frame the clouded blue—a new pair of glasses, brown rims versus the jade she wore in Paris. Unbidden, my hand pats the inner pocket of my jacket over my right pec, reassuring myself of its contents.

"It's not mine; it's yours." My eyes roll heavenward where a thick canopy of bare branches form a gloomy barrier to the sky above.

What is wrong with this woman?

She should be overjoyed by her new financial freedom. Most women love to shop. They buy fancy trinkets and expensive clothing as status symbols. And while Allison may not be a socialite, she's still a woman. I find it hard to believe there isn't something she wants. Something money can easily purchase.

"Fine, *my* money," she acquiesces, an indignant spark lighting her eyes. It's the first time a glimmer of annoyance has revealed itself, proving she's not all terrified glances and uneasy breaths. "Despite your email, I've been skeptical that it's real, which has made me hold off on spending more of it. But as far as the apartment, it would be a waste of money to pay the fee to break the lease when I can stick it out for a couple more months."

"Are you serious right now? An extra thousand or two to get out of your lease is nothing compared to what you have."

"Old habits die hard when you've struggled your entire life. I can't suddenly be okay with dropping a ton of cash when it's not necessary," she grumbles, spearing me with a judgmental glare.

"How much?"

"What?"

I pull my phone out and draft a text to my accountant. "How. Much?"

"For what?"

"For you to feel comfortable ending the lease and moving somewhere better than this." I wave a hand toward the shabby apartments. They're not exactly derelict, but Allison can do better.

"Um... Nothing. There isn't a number."

"Fine, I'll decide for myself." I tell John to deposit another million dollars into her account immediately. A minute later, there's a ding, and she checks the notification.

"Are you freaking kidding me?" Her gaze lifts to meet mine. "You added more money."

And I'll add more if necessary.

"That should be enough to cover your reluctance to pay whatever the fee is. Why don't you show me what the inside of these monstrosities look like?"

My return flight takes off in another hour. This impromptu trip was ill-advised.

I have a meeting with my lawyers concerning next steps with Petit Enterprises now that it's under new ownership, but I can't resist the opportunity to stay a little longer.

To steal another peek into her life.

Because the woman is a conundrum.

A Rubik's cube of mystery.

It's a damn shame I'm a fucking problem-solver or else I could let this inconvenient fascination go.

Allison laughs in disbelief. "You came here from god-knows-where to give me more money and judge my apartment? I'm the one who saved *your* life, remember? I should be the one calling the shots."

That draws a chuckle from me. The idea of this woman running my life is beyond comprehension. "*Fille folle...* You'll learn soon enough that I'm the only one in control here. Hustle your cute ass back to the apartment, or find out exactly how far I'm willing to go to get what I want."

Like tossing her over my shoulder and hauling her upstairs myself.

Being careful of her recent injuries, of course.

It shouldn't matter what her apartment looks like. It won't be her home for much longer, but I want to learn more about Allison. Maybe the interior will offer clues to explain her strange behavior.

She shuffles backward, darting a worried glance between me and the apartment building. *Ah, my scared little rabbit is back.* "Now's not a good time. You heard the dogs. They don't like strangers."

"They'll learn to like me." My hand drops to the small of her back to push her in the direction of the stairs. Her shoulders slump in defeat, and whatever frustration that flared to life earlier evaporates like it never existed.

Gone is her previous stance of defiance.

In its place is the nervous bunny again.

What is she hiding up there?

CHAPTER NINE

MATHIAS

It doesn't take long to figure out why she was so hesitant.

The stench of dogs, urine, and manufactured vanilla hits me as soon as I step inside the apartment after Allison locks the dogs away in her roommate's room.

Dirty dishes lay scattered around the kitchen while tufts of gray fur form an army of dust bunnies on the floor. A black cat saunters out of a door that lets out a little jingle from the bell on the knob, and the smell of piss becomes stronger.

What the fuck is Allison doing still living here?

Because this is far worse than I imagined.

I thought I'd find outdated appliances and peeling paint—and those things exist, but they're not the most pressing reason why it's unsafe to stay. It's the beginning of a *Hoarders* episode that concerns me most.

My attention snaps to Allison, ready to point out the ridiculousness of forgoing a nice, clean apartment for this dump, when the watery haze filming her eyes stops me in my tracks. Shame pours from her hunched body as if waiting for the humiliating blow of my judgment, and I take a moment to study the apartment again.

Yes, paper plates with half-eaten pizza crusts are stacked on the counter, but a tied trash bag rests against a kitchen cabinet. Rubber gloves and a sponge rest beside the full sink, soap bubbles attesting to the fact that they were recently used.

And yes, the overwhelming aroma of animals and a dirty litter box speaks to a lack of care, but then there's a vanilla candle flickering on the coffee table attempting to mask it all. Kitschy artwork and knickknacks decorate the walls and furniture as if someone tried to create a cozy home amidst the chaotic mess.

"Would you rather go back outside?" she asks quietly, her knuckles white as she hugs tight fists around her waist.

"No, here's fine." There's a softness in my tone that I've never heard before, but it feels like speaking above a soothing baritone might shatter the fragility draping Allison. "Where do you sleep?"

"At the end of the hall." She points to a closed door where a cheerful Valentine's Day sign hangs over the back. It's out of season now, but clearly, that's the least of her problems.

Striding toward the room, I notice the other three doors in the hall are closed as well, and I wonder what state of disarray they're hiding.

Bits of glitter fall off the cheap sign as I swing the door wide and get my first glimpse of Allison's room.

It smells fresher here. A window by her bed lets in a cool breeze, and there's one of those fragrance plug-ins on the wall by her nightstand.

The cat follows us inside and hops onto the mattress, turning in a circle before plopping down on the comforter and promptly beginning to bathe its paw.

It seems Allison isn't the main contributor to the mess outside her room, since there looks to be attempts at being neat. Folded clothes, bed made, ensuite bathroom counter clear.

Though there are still spots of half-done chores.

I'm not judging her, but the lack of cleanliness worries me. I don't want her living this way. Especially when it can't be healthy breathing in the dust and animal byproducts floating in the air.

Allison gathers a small pile of clothing from the desk in the corner and hurries to a packed walk-in closet.

"Sorry for the mess. If I'd known you were coming by, I would have..."

I raise my hand to cut her off. "An apology isn't necessary. Just tell me what you need." It's not what I expected to say, but it feels right. Allison obviously requires help. It's just a matter of figuring out what is top priority.

"Need?" Her brow wrinkles. Like no one has ever asked how best to support her before.

I wouldn't have guessed that was her background. Sure, she didn't grow up in a sick bastard's makeshift mercenary school like me, but I figured she had a semblance of a happy childhood based on her past academic achievements and two parents who were still married rather than divorced.

Obviously, I was wrong, and those didn't count for shit.

My hands cover hers where they're fiddling with an empty water bottle from the nightstand, and she freezes at the contact. Her face remains averted, until I gently hook her chin between thumb and forefinger and guide it upward.

"Don't deny something is amiss here, so what do you need?" I
don't know why I'm pushing this. Don't know why it matters to
me. If Allison wants to live life harder than she has to, that's her
prerogative. It has absolutely nothing to do with me.

Yet I'm in Raleigh after chartering the jet to check on her.

Why?

She's a puzzle, and you itch to solve them.

That's the only reason.

"I—"

The reaction I was trying to avoid earlier finally comes as tears
stream down Allison's flushed cheeks. Her silent cries rattle the
chain wrapped tightly around the gnashing beast I keep buried
deep unless someone fucks with me or my brothers.

So why is it waking for Allison?

Why does she affect me so easily?

"I need help," she admits with a shudder.

Words spill from her like a flood, matching the increasing pace
of each tear as her face gleams with resignation. The guarded
walls she kept high and barbed-wired crumble like they were
made from a stack of playing cards—one pointed blow and
they came tumbling down.

"I'm so tired. So overwhelmed. Even when I thought about
using the money to hire a maid service, I couldn't do it. There's
so much to do, and it's embarrassing. Every website said they
didn't deal with clutter, which is half the problem. I tried to
clean and organize, and I got some done but then..." More quiet
sobs fall as she chokes on her words.

"What about your roommate?"

Allison sighs and deflates, though my grasp keeps her gaze on
me.

"Bailey..." She bites her lip, contemplating the question. "Since she's dealing with her own mental health stuff, she doesn't think she should have to help. Which I get, but everything's become a nightmare since she lost her job. She and the pets depend on me for everything at this point, and even with your money, I can't do anything. I'm stuck. Burnt out."

"I wish I had someone who could..." She stops and shakes her head at the unspoken thought. "Nevermind. It's selfish."

"You wish you had someone to assume control. Take care of you. Shoulder the heavy burden you've placed on yourself without a second thought."

Blood pounds in my ears.

In my heart.

In my cock.

The air charges around us, and it requires all of my willpower to remain outwardly calm, despite the feral hunger Allison's half-voiced admission ignites.

Don't take the bait.

You didn't come to North Carolina for this.

"How did you...?" Wonder shines through the tears before she shakes it off, swiping at a few salty droplets. "It's a foolish dream. I don't want to burden another person with my messy life. Everyone has problems, and I'll deal with mine like I always have." A tremulous smile forces its way onto her lips, and I growl at the brave facade she's trying to project.

I don't want fake positivity.

I don't want lies.

"No, Angel, you won't." I studiously ignore the endearment that slips out and continue, "You saved my life. It's time I save yours."

A watery laugh trembles from her throat. "I'm not dying. Just having a tough time. It'll pass."

"Agreed. Forget about calling the maid service or breaking your lease. I'll handle things from now on."

My brothers hate my impulse to lead. My need to control a situation. We're independent men with our own unique skill sets, but that doesn't mean I'm content sitting back when someone should captain the ship.

I had so little control growing up with Conrad dictating my every move. No autonomy from the moment my mom pawned me off on him.

"I can't let you do that. Not when it's my responsibility. It's too generous."

"No one has ever accused me of being generous in my life. You think it's selfish to ask for help and receive it? For me to bear the mental load for you? I've got news for you, Allie Angel." I tighten my hold on her chin and dip my head lower so she breathes in the rasp of my words. Lets them sink so deeply into her soul that she knows I'm serious. "I'm the fucking selfish one. You just offered a starving lion his first glimpse of a succulent gazelle."

My body backs Allison into the wall as I allow her to see the dark craving in my expression. Rational thought has fled the scene. I'm acting on pure instinct now.

"And I'm greedy for a taste."

"Y... you are?" Her chest hitches as my lips skim along her jawline to the pulse racing in her neck. I savor the sweet rush of power it fills me with. So vulnerable. So ripe for the taking.

That may not have been the plan upon landing in Raleigh, but I'm an adaptable man, especially when it comes to claiming something I want.

"I want your submission, *ma cherie*, and you offered it to me on a silver platter." It may not have been what she had in mind when she voiced her secret desire, but it was at the core of her request.

Allison is a strong woman; I don't doubt her strength.

She's brave; I witnessed it firsthand.

But my guardian angel is also weary. Bogged down by more than she's shared so far I'd wager. So overwhelmed that even the simplest of tasks seems daunting.

She said it herself—she needs help.

And I'm just the man to give it to her.

CHAPTER TEN

ALLISON

Mathias's offer shouldn't tempt me.

What intelligent woman would gladly put herself in a man's hands so completely?

He's not my boyfriend. Not my husband. This is only the second time we've spoken, if I don't count our brief email exchange.

Yet I know I'll give in.

Forget my initial fear of the sort of people he may be mixed up with. Maybe the drive-by had nothing to do with him personally. Maybe it was just a random act of violence.

Either way, I'm too far gone to fight him when he's promising to give me exactly what I've wanted for years. Too numb and apathetic about my life to put up much of a protest.

After decades of always being the adult in relationships—for family, for Bailey—this is my chance to be free. In the past, if I ever took a risk and stumbled, no one would've caught me. No one would've been there to offer advice. The only person I've ever been able to count on is me.

And it's driven me to the brink of a mental breakdown as stress and hopelessness built upon one another and formed an inescapable pit. Thoughts of suicide have flickered to life in my darkest moments, so where's the harm in following Mathias's lead?

I may be screwed, but at least there's a chance of happiness with his aid. I can't say the same if I remain alone here.

"Okay," I murmur, tilting my head enough to feel his lips graze my cheek. The rough brush of his beard is a lightning bolt to my nerves.

God, I'm so touch-starved that the barest caress from a stranger sends my body into instant alert.

"I wasn't asking for your permission, Allie, but your compliance is appreciated. I'll schedule a cleaning service to come by, along with a packing crew for the move."

"I can't leave Bailey. She hasn't found a stable job yet and needs..."

"How long has she been searching?"

I don't want to tell him. It'll reveal how weak I've been. *He already knows.*

"Over a year."

"Are you fucking kidding me?" A rumble of anger vibrates from his chest. Ever the primal lion in his analogy. "You've been paying for everything this entire time?"

I simply nod, knowing how terrible it sounds.

Bailey and I have been friends since freshman year of college. We've always said we're bonded for life. But after she got laid off, she just gave up. Started spouting off rants about end-stage capitalism and how she refused to contribute to the system.

Which, to each her own, but it seemed insensitive when I was still expected to work *in the system* if we wanted a roof over our heads and food for us and her pets.

Every time she 'lowered' herself to start a new job to bring in some cash, whether it was as a waitress or cashier, Bailey inevitably quit within a week, citing a myriad of reasons for the decision.

Toxic work environment.

Not enough money.

Mathias drags a hand through his hair, irritation flashing in his steely eyes. "*Putain de merde*! Yet you still left the money untouched. *De toutes les bêtises*... You require a firm hand to make decisions for your benefit, don't you?"

I don't answer. Too distracted by him speaking French. It rolls off the tongue and sounds sexy as hell in his gravelly tone.

I shouldn't find anything about him sexy. He's still a stranger. A potentially dangerous one.

And he's the man I'm giving myself to.

Bailey won't be happy to hear I'm moving out, even if I plan on leaving her with enough money to stay in the apartment until the lease ends. Maybe it makes me a bitch using Mathias as an excuse, but a weight lifts at being able to blame him for whatever fallout there is.

Like I'm not the one making the decision, so she can't blame me.

Even though he's doing what I would do if I wasn't too overwhelmed, scared, and too damn numb.

Always numb.

Always alone.

I should probably talk to my doctor about upping my medication, but again, that's one more task that seems impossible to accomplish.

"Pack a bag. This is the last time you'll see this apartment," Mathias says as he pulls out his phone and starts rapidly typing on the screen.

"I can't just disappear. I need to talk to Bailey and pack more than a bag. I can't leave yet."

"Yes, you can, and you are. Professionals will handle everything from here on out. And if they fuck up your stuff, they'll regret it." He spares a glance at me before returning to his phone. "You've got ten minutes to gather whatever is coming with you today. The rest will come later."

I debate disagreeing with him, but when have I ever chosen to argue?

Never.

Besides, Mathias bulldozes his way through conversations until he gets what he wants, which should irk the hell out of me, but instead, it provides a sense of peace.

Maybe I'll feel differently if we ever truly disagree on a subject, but so far, he's only pushing me to accept what I desperately want but refuse out of fear.

The money for a fresh start in life.

Cutting ties with Bailey.

Hurrying to the closet, I drag my suitcase out and dump it on the bed since it's still full from the trip to Paris. I've been meaning to empty it and wash the worn clothes, but I never got around to it.

As I mentally check off the necessities—shampoo, conditioner, toothbrush, underwear, socks, phone charger—a frenzy begins behind the door to Bailey's room, alerting us to her arrival before she stomps through the front door.

"Where the hell are Roscoe and Palmer?" She drops her purse on the overflowing bench we have in the entry and kicks off her shoes.

"I'll deal with her. You finish packing." Mathias edges me aside to face off with Bailey.

Oh, no.

It takes me a couple of tries to zip the stuffed suitcase closed, due to shaky hands, but once it's sealed, I swing it onto the floor and race out to the living room, forgetting to spare a final glance toward the bedroom I've slept in for the past five years.

"Who the fuck are you?" Bailey's high-pitched screech sends the dogs into a barking fit. They're desperate to burst free from confinement and protect their owner.

Frankly, I'm surprised the thin plywood door is holding them back. They're both large enough to break through if necessary.

"Who I am is irrelevant. All you need to know is that your free ride ends today. Allie is leaving, and you won't be seeing her again. If you try to contact her, attempt to guilt her into saving your lazy ass again, you won't like what happens," Mathias growls, and I swear I might swoon on the stained carpet.

This man is taking his job seriously, and another round of tears threatens to unleash because of it. When was the last time someone stood up for me? *Literally never.* So, this is a welcome change, even if I should be wary of him.

"Allison?" Bailey's eyes find me striding down the hallway. I attempt to pass Mathias, but he shoots an arm out to block my path.

"Stay behind me," he warns. Tension ripples over his sharp features and broad shoulders. An avenging angel. *For me.*

A shiver of pleasure raises goosebumps on my skin, but I can't let him deal with Bailey alone. "It's fine. She's not going to hurt me." I try again to shove forward.

Mathias widens his stance and glares down at me. "I said, 'Stay. Behind. Me.'" The low command ignites a flare of heat in my veins. No one has ever been this protective of me.

I'm always the self-soothing, self-reliant, *self-everything* person. It's my duty to protect them, not the other way around.

"Allison, seriously... What is going on? Who is this guy, and why is he acting like you're some kind of domestic victim escaping abuse?"

"Because she is," Mathias says, taking an intimidating step closer to Bailey. "Allison bore the burden of caring for you and your menagerie of animals for years, and you've let her, despite the detrimental effect it's had on her. You may not have caused physical harm, but you've done damage. I don't know if you're a selfish bitch, or maybe you're truly dumb and blind enough to not see it. Either way, this ends now. Get off your fucking ass and take responsibility for your life. No one else is going to do it for you. And Allison sure as hell isn't going to shield you from the consequences of your actions anymore."

He turns to me and wrests the suitcase handle out of my hand. "Let's go. We're done here."

I nod, dumbstruck by his fervid defense and struggling to figure out what to say as we walk by Bailey. We've been friends for a long time. Shouldn't there be a final farewell? A proper closing to our friendship?

Mathias handled it for you.

Just like he said he would.

I meet Bailey's pissed glower and sigh in acceptance. Our connection is severed. I'm no longer trapped. I'll send the money to complete the lease because of who I am not because of who she is, then that will be the end of it.

The winter chill washes over me like a refreshing dip in the pool on a summer's day. If Mathias didn't have a hold on my hand, I'd likely soar into the sky, free as a bird.

Because that's how I feel—*free*.

Even if I needed to put myself in Mathias's hands to get there.

CHAPTER ELEVEN

MATHIAS

We arrive at the private airstrip twenty minutes later, and that's when Allison breaks the quiet contemplation she fell into after we left her apartment.

"Why are we here?" she asks, nervously sipping the bottled water I gave her earlier.

"To fly to Boston." I finish emailing my lawyers that we need to push our meeting to later tonight. Once we arrive in Boston, I'll need to get Allie settled before heading into the office.

"What? I thought we were driving to a new apartment complex. Not leaving the state! People will worry. My coworkers, friends."

"You mean friends like Bailey who take advantage of you, or the ones from Paris who deserted you after you were fucking shot?" I don't pussyfoot around with laying out the facts. Allie's life needs an overhaul from the living situation to her friends. Although a group of men known as the Blackchapel Bastards may not be a good replacement, it's what she's got.

"Oh my god." She drops her head in her hands. "Those were my coworkers, and they came to the hospital after you left."

"They should have been by your side from the start," I retort. "You gave yourself to me, remember? My job would be impossible with hundreds of miles between us. In Boston, I can make sure you're properly taken care of."

"So... what? I remain holed up at a hotel for the foreseeable future?"

"Don't be ridiculous," I scoff as a text vibrates with confirmation for the evening's meeting time. "I'm not stashing you in a hotel. You're staying at Blackchapel Manor with me. And it's not like you're a prisoner. You have two million dollars in your bank account. Figure out what you want to do, and do it."

"This is too much," she groans. Her knee bounces, bumping into the door with a rhythmic thump, until I drop a hand over her lap to stop the movement before she bruises herself.

Our driver unloads the trunk and gives Allie's suitcase to Kurie, the flight attendant, who rolls it to the undercarriage storage. The pilot greets us at the bottom of the short staircase leading into the fuselage, and soon we're buckled into the large leather seats as the plane speeds down the runway.

Once we're airborne, I signal Kurie for snacks.

"Have you eaten today?"

Allison's curious gaze roams around the cabin before landing on me. "Yes, of course." She says it like it should be obvious, but there's a shift in her demeanor, and immediately, warning bells go off in my head.

"Let me rephrase: What exactly did you eat? And don't lie to me."

She fidgets uncomfortably in her seat, so I reach across the empty space between us to unbuckle her seatbelt and drag her into my lap. It's an awkward tug of war as she wiggles beneath my hands in protest.

My fingertips dig into her soft love handles hard enough to leave marks.

"Enough," I command. "If I want you in my lap, then that's where you're damn well going to be. Perhaps it'll make you think twice before trying to lie to me, either outright or by omission."

She freezes in my arms, her lush body conforming to my sharp angles, and I fight the temptation to forget my plan for food and skip straight to devouring *her*. It's been a while since I last fucked a woman—I've been too busy brokering the Petit deal to bother with sex—but Allie's generous weight in my lap, her sweet scent teasing my nose, has me ready to break months of celibacy.

"I'm not your roommate or whoever else required kid gloves. I'm the man you've relinquished control to. In *every* aspect of your life, Angel, and I don't do anything in half-measures. Something you ought to learn quickly unless you're ready to face the consequences of disobeying me."

Despite the warning, one of these days, she'll do exactly that. It's inevitable, and I can't wait to see the red imprint of my hand on her ass.

Today, Allie is too raw and fragile from what she's been through. She needs time and space to adjust to her new circumstances.

But there's a limit to what I'll accept, and Allie lying to me is a hard one.

"A frozen breakfast burrito and coffee."

"And lunch?"

I can tell she doesn't want to tell me. It's in the way she tries to curl into a little ball as if making herself smaller will ever be able to hide her from me.

"Lunch?" I repeat more firmly.

"A handful of trail mix," she mumbles. "I was in the middle of emptying the sink and didn't want to mess up my groove by stopping. Then I got distracted because the dishwasher was already full which meant I needed to put those dishes away first. And... I couldn't bring myself to make lunch. It felt like too much work."

My palm cups her jaw, and the anxious clenching of muscles there is a beacon for my thumb as I gently massage the area. A woman as soft as Allison shouldn't be consumed by tension. Shouldn't be rigid and strained.

She should be languid and relaxed because of how safe and content she feels.

And that's exactly my goal.

I've fantasized about having something of my own. Growing up with six other boys in a strict prison-like environment, it was one of my favorite dreams to pull out and examine before stuffing the desire deep inside.

The problem with owning something—*or someone*—is the worry over losing it.

Conrad refused to let us get attached to anything. Even the brotherhood that formed between us had to be carefully concealed with apathy and nonchalance.

I don't have Conrad waiting in the wings to snatch Allison from me, but I do have enemies. All of the Blackchapel Bastards do, yet I took her anyway.

What's the point of being the master of my world if I can't do whatever the fuck I want? If that means claiming Allison completely and owning her submission, then I'm damn well going to do it.

Kurie discreetly unfolds the hidden table to our right and delivers a circular charcuterie board filled with fruits, cheeses, and a variety of meats before retreating.

Plucking a purple grape and a triangle of gruyere from the selection, I raise it to Allison's mouth.

"That won't happen again. If I'm not around to personally ensure you're eating, one of my brothers will be, along with our housekeeper, Mrs. Shandy. Now, eat." Allie stares between me and the food hovering in front of her before tentatively accepting the offering, her lips parting an inch to let me feed her.

"Good girl," I murmur, warmth spreading through my chest with each bite she takes from me.

I've never fed a woman with my own hand before. I've limited my desire for dominance to the confines of the bedroom, after specifically arranging for women who understood the score—no-strings-attached sex.

Let me control the scene, and I'll guarantee your pleasure. But nothing extended past the four walls of whatever hotel suite I reserved for the evening.

The type of relationship I'm interested in isn't for the casual hook-up, and frankly, it hasn't been a priority to explore that side of myself within something more permanent. I have my father to take down, along with the rest of The Syndicate. Revenge has been the motivating factor in my life—not settling down.

I wasn't lying when I told Allie how starved I am for an arrangement like this. We skipped the slow build-up of trust and dove headfirst into what amounts to a binding verbal contract in my mind.

Allison proved her trustworthiness by saving my life.

I will repay the favor tenfold by tending to her every need.

In return, the beast inside me that craves the privilege of a woman's submission—craves *Allie's* submission—will be satisfied.

I will finally have something of my own. *Someone who is all mine.*

For the next few minutes, we continue the process of me choosing her next bite, and Allie quietly accepting it, until she hesitantly stops my wrist and reaches for one of the small bottles of water Kurie left behind with the food.

She swallows a couple of gulps. "Can I ask you something?"

"Go ahead."

"I know you're on the board of Blackchapel Inc., but is that all? Maybe I've seen too many movies, but that drive-by seemed meant for you, and it worries me that I might be getting involved with someone who's..." Her teeth nibble her bottom lip as she searches for the right words. "Bad for me."

"Make no mistake. I *am* bad for you, but it's too late to turn back now." *You're mine.* The decision to bring her into my life might as well be written in stone, but I debate how much to share about my world.

She'll learn soon enough at the manor.

"My brothers and I run Blackchapel Incorporated, but that's just a means to an end. Our true purpose is more complicated. The incident in Paris was targeted toward Luca, the man who was with me. His dad arranged it."

Allie jerks back. "His dad? Isn't he your dad, too?"

"No. None of us are blood-related, except for Dmitri and Aleksei. Our bond goes deeper than blood because of how we were raised. We're the illegitimate sons of men who run an organized crime ring known as The Syndicate. I'll spare you the details, but my brothers and I are determined to bring down the organization and ruin our bastard fathers."

At my admission, her brows practically reach her hairline as she fidgets in my lap.

"I understand the need for retribution after a troubled childhood, but wouldn't it be easier to move on? It seems too dangerous to challenge a crime ring when there are so few of you. I mean I don't know how many brothers you have, but I doubt it's enough to crush something as ominous sounding as The Syndicate."

"There are seven of us, and we're known as the Blackchapel Bastards because of our ruthless reputations," I say. "Blackchapel Inc. is the legitimate side of our dealings. Its criminal underbelly is Blackthorn, a legion of men loyal to us and our cause, so you don't need to worry. Decades of training is in our veins. You'll be kept safe. I promise you that."

We've turned Blackchapel Manor into a monolith of security measures. No one is getting within an inch of the property without us knowing about it.

Which is why my little angel will remain behind its ivy-covered walls until I arrange for her security detail.

I'm not taking any chances of someone stealing her away from me.

CHAPTER TWELVE

LUCA D'AMORA

When I asked Mathias about 'his girl,' I was mostly fucking with him. The woman checked out as nothing more than a good Samaritan, which was why Mathias's constant monitoring of her was hilarious.

I didn't expect the bastard to bring her back to Blackchapel like a damn orphan puppy.

Another message updating me on Allie's arrival to the manor lights up my phone.

RAFE: *I can't believe you're missing this. Where are you?*

Ignoring him, I consider this latest development with Mathias. He's our group's unofficial leader, and he's usually calm and controlled. Rash decisions aren't his typical MO, yet he flew Allison from North Carolina to Massachusetts on a fucking whim. As if we don't have enough going on with our plan to ruin The Syndicate. As if the danger we're constantly in is the perfect place for a woman.

Pot meet kettle.

These are warnings I've told myself, but it's not like I'm actually putting Eden in harm's way. I haven't even talked to her.

I sit in the tree that looks into the large windows of her living room. *That's all.* There's distance between us, one that provides a buffer of safety.

Because my life is a shitshow.

My father tried to kill me in Paris. We traced the license plates of the van involved to a couple of low-level goons in his organization, and there's no way they would've gone rogue—assassinating their boss's illegitimate son for fun. That would mean a quick trip to the morgue.

A lamp flashes to life, and I shove thoughts of Enzo D'Amora aside in favor of watching my favorite girl.

Eden Marino.

Sweet and innocent with so many curves it would take me days to explore them all. Not that I'll get the chance anytime soon.

For now, I'm content to watch and wait. Bide my time until it's safe to bring Eden home to the manor.

Obviously, my thinking is clearer than Mathias's at the moment.

I smirk.

Maybe *I* should be the Blackchapel Bastards' unofficial leader.

CHAPTER THIRTEEN

ALLISON

So, this is what happens when intrusive thoughts win.

My life gets hijacked by a wealthy mercenary, and I become his—*Pet? Submissive? Mistress?* I'm not clear on what he expects in return for his protection—while he installs me in this enormous mansion on the outskirts of Boston.

After introducing three of the other six men who live at Blackchapel Manor—Rafael, Jonah, and Hugo, formidable men wearing varying degrees of confused expressions—Mathias showed me to a beautiful room upstairs in the East Wing. Because, of course, his home is large enough to have freaking wings.

The king-sized bed I'm currently lounging in dominates one wall while the bank of windows to its right offers an aerial view of the sleeping gardens. I'm sure summer sunrises are something to behold as the warm golden light splashes over flowers and shrubs before sweeping up the manor to brighten my room.

It's unfortunate I won't be here to see it. Mathias will surely tire of our arrangement by then.

"Then I'll be on my own again," I whisper into the empty room.

For hours, I've been floating in an odd dream state—from Mathias first appearing on my doorstep to the flight where he fed me while I sat in his lap to now lying awake in bed, staring up at the high ceiling, exhausted yet jittery.

The crash after a tumultuous day.

The perfect time for my mind to spiral and drag my poor body with it.

Where's that numb cocoon when I need it?

"A is for apple. B is for bank. C is for cash." I list each letter in the alphabet along with whatever corresponding word pops into my head. It's supposed to distract my thoughts so they don't fixate on worrying, but I've run through the alphabet three times so far with no change.

An itch continues to tingle along my skin. My heart pounds in my chest. In my ears. Never lessening, only heightening. Nausea roils around in my stomach, and chills threaten to turn me into a quivering mess.

All signs point to an anxiety attack gearing up for a full-scale assault, so I toss the blankets off to search for the emergency prescription that's meant to curb the symptoms when they become too much.

My feet sink into the thick rug covering most of the room's hardwood flooring as I stumble through the dark and search for my suitcase.

What was I thinking leaving my home—*the fucking state*—with a stranger?

A man who intimidated and interrogated me in Paris.

Yes, he caught me in a vulnerable position earlier, but I'm not a reckless person—no matter how often I wish I could be. Have I fantasized about being whisked away from my problems? Of course. Who hasn't?

But you're not supposed to actually let a bossy stranger dictate your life. Even if it does monumentally suck.

You're not supposed to accept his control. Not supposed to willingly give in to it.

I'm not an idiot, but right now, I feel like the world's dumbest woman. They'll feature me on that show *1000 Stupid Ways to Die*, and I'll be number one. The pathetic girl who was brave enough to take a bullet for a man but too weak to handle her own life.

"Come on... Where are you?" My hands dig through the hastily packed suitcase by the door, rooting around for my plastic-container lifeline. Tears prick behind my eyelids as my vision blurs.

Where is it?

Did I forget to pack it?

What am I going to do?

There are a few options I can try to calm my nervous system, like a hot shower or playing the town-building game on my phone, but those usually aren't strong enough to completely mitigate an attack. I know because my therapist asked me to rank the effectiveness of my coping mechanisms once.

Hot shower = 3 points

Mobile game = 2 points

Drawing figure-eights = 1 point

The idea was to see what worked then adding items together to create an even powerful coping method. Technically, my shower and game would equal five points out of ten, but five measly points isn't going to cut it against a level twenty attack.

"I wish my space heater was here." That thing is worth ten points because it wards off the anxiety chills. Some might think it's ridiculous, but I even use it during the summer when it's ninety degrees outside because my body doesn't care what the weather is like.

If my fucked-up brain chemistry says it's freezing, then I'm freezing, and shivering uncontrollably is the answer.

"Oh, thank god." The tumble of pills is music to my ears as my fingers wrap around the medication. I quickly pop one in my mouth and rush to the bathroom to drink some water from my cupped hands.

Water splashes on the counter from the improvised cup, and small droplets join the puddles as I lean over the sink, tired tears slowly sliding down my cheeks to plop on the marble.

I'm so sick of this.

A gleam of silver catches my eye. There's a shaving blade resting in a leather placket in the corner of the double vanity.

How considerate of Mathias to provide guests with fancy shaving implements.

Curious, I unroll the leather and remove the straight razor from its restraint.

It flicks open with an easy snick.

The sharp metal mesmerizes me as it reflects my distorted image.

A thundering roar blares in my ears as my gaze focuses on the object in my hand, imagining how painful a slice from its blade would be. Picturing perfectly round beads of blood dripping down the edge.

It soothes something in me. Something wild and dark and melancholic to the extreme.

Inhaling deeply, I hold the breath and gently bring the point of the razor to my inner wrist. Two prominent lines slash below the palm, symmetrical guidelines that my fuzzy brain appreciates.

A is for agony.

B is for blue.

C is for cold.

D is for death.

"What the hell are you doing?"

In a flash, the blade clatters to the floor as Mathias storms into the bathroom. Fire and fear form a molten glare in his diamond-hard eyes, frightening me in their intensity.

I stumble backward and bang into the glass shower wall.

Mathias pauses, glances at the fallen razor, then burns me with another penetrating stare. "What were you doing, Allie? If I hadn't seen the light under the door..."

"I'd be fine."

I've never gone too far in the past, and it wasn't in my plan tonight. *But the thought...* The thought of hurting myself was a welcome distraction to the actual war going on in my body and mind.

"The damn razor was over your wrist. It was touching your skin." He snags my limp wrist and raises it between us. His hold is surprisingly gentle considering the fury radiating from his body, but his carefulness doesn't cause the fear in my veins to stall.

No, it's gathering momentum, combining with the other fears thrashing my insides.

I swallow hard, willing myself to calm down.

Telling myself to do so has never worked in the past, but I really don't want to break down in front of Mathias again.

Once today is my limit.

"That's as far as it was going to go. I promise."

Mathias runs a free hand through his ruffled hair. Did I wake him? Where did he come from?

"How are you here?" I ask, hoping to distract him.

"We share adjoining rooms. When the manor was originally built, these were the master and mistress suites." He tugs me toward a door I hadn't noticed before, flipping off the bathroom lights as we pass into my room's twin—except for the bed. Somehow his is even larger than mine.

My footsteps stutter over another plush rug, but Mathias keeps pulling until we're both tucked into his bed, his broad chest to my rigid back.

"Tell me what I walked into," he murmurs, the warmth of his breath tickling my ear.

The medicine I took has taken some of the edge off my anxiety, but it's going to be a few hours before I'm calm enough to sleep. Which means there's no escape from Mathias's questioning.

"I shouldn't be here. I want to go home." It's not an answer to his question, but it's the best I can do.

Bailey may not be a good friend, and ours may not be a healthy friendship or living situation, but at least it's familiar. Safe because I know what to expect.

"This was a mistake. I never should have agreed to whatever this is, and I definitely shouldn't have gotten on that jet."

"You're scared." His arm tightens around my waist, putting pressure on my belly. "I understand your apprehension. What I don't get is how that translates to the scene I witnessed in the bathroom."

"I'm having an anxiety attack."

There I said it.

It's not a crime or something to be ashamed of, but I hate having to admit it aloud.

"Everything hit me at once in an overwhelming wave. And I'm sick of dealing with it. Do you know how exhausting it is to manage your mental health? To try to do the right things to get better and still suffer setbacks?" The words are a stuttering, wobbly mess as my crying starts up again. "Sometimes the imagined relief of... not existing... helps dampen the pain."

Silence meets the end of my explanation. Mathias's heavy breathing is slow and steady, and I consciously try to match the rhythm.

"How often does this happen?" he quietly asks.

"Anxiety attacks? They used to be more frequent before I started therapy and medication. Now, it's every once in a while. The thoughts of being gone?" Another euphemism for suicide since saying the word out loud makes it too real. "More often."

"Fuck, Angel... When I accused you of lacking a preservation instinct, I didn't realize you had a literal death wish."

"I don't," I deny. "Thoughts help; actions aren't necessary. I don't actually want to hurt myself. I hate pain and avoid it at all costs, which is why I avoided confrontations with Bailey." And with my parents and brother. People that I've discussed with my therapist about going 'no contact' with but have never had the guts to follow through on.

Because of the fallout.

The guilt trips that would await me.

The hurt feelings on both sides.

Any improvement to my mental health from 'no contact' would be demolished by the repercussions.

Mathias sighs and buries his lips in my hair, his beard tangling with the curls and causing intermittent pulling sensations. "This conversation isn't over, but it's late, and you need sleep. Are you feeling any better?"

"Slightly. I took something about twenty minutes ago, but it's not always foolproof."

"What can I do? Aside from flying you back to North Carolina, that is. Because there's no way in hell I'm letting you go now that I know how badly you need me."

A sliver of amusement works its way through me. "You think very highly of yourself. I realize I don't have the best track record with you, but I've been taking care of myself for almost thirty years just fine."

"Our definitions of 'just fine' are vastly different." His leg covers mine as his arms squeeze tighter, forming a solid nest of heat and muscle. "I read once that deep pressure can regulate the nervous system. Let's see if it's true, hmm?"

Nodding in agreement, because that's why I own a weighted blanket currently crumpled at the end of my bed back home, my attention returns to slowing my breaths, mirroring Mathias's relaxed inhales and exhales until darkness finally wins the battle for my mind.

CHAPTER FOURTEEN

MATHIAS

It takes a long time for me to fall asleep.

Nothing could have prepared me for the scene I walked into: Allison standing frozen in the bathroom, her eyes unfocused, and my straight razor poised to cut across her vulnerable wrist. If I hadn't already been awake questioning the wisdom of placing her in a separate room rather than demanding she stay in mine, I may never have noticed when the bathroom light appeared beneath the closed door. Allison would have been alone with her thoughts, and who knows what would have happened?

My grip tightens, and I take comfort in the evidence of her life. Warm skin, steady heartbeat. Her chills stopped around the time I finally felt the tension leave her body an hour ago.

For the first time in my life, a sense of helplessness creeps into my psyche, because as much as I'd like to, I can't control this.

I wanted to stop her pain. The shivering. The tears. The mental battle in her head. But all I could do was hold her while she suffered. Until exhaustion won out.

It's unacceptable, considering my promise to care for her needs. In the morning, I plan on hearing the full extent of her troubles, since my gut is telling me they extend beyond a bad roommate. I'm going to learn what medications she's on, who her therapist is, and how often she sees them.

Then I'm going to make a plan.

***

When the sun rises, it brings with it the heady realization that Allie's plump ass is cradling my morning wood, and this may be the best way I've ever woken up.

My dreams centered on her holding a knife, twirling it between her fingers, while my father laughed from the sidelines, a gun trained on me to prevent my interference as the flashing blade nicked her skin over and over again.

To say I could use the relief Allie's curvy body snuggled against mine provides is an understatement.

My palm slips beneath her tee and slides higher to cup her breast, the generous swell overflowing the possessive grasp. My hand contracts causing her nipple to push between two fingers, and I wish we were positioned differently so I could suck the stiffening bud into my mouth.

Allie shifts but remains sleeping as I massage her breast while working my other hand into her sleep shorts to trace the hot seam of her pussy. My dick is rock hard as I slowly grind into her ass, a rumble of need vibrating in my chest.

Maybe it's wrong to touch her after such a harrowing night, but I can't help myself. She feels too good when I've been craving more since our agreement yesterday. After her lush curves molded to my lap while I fed her. After chaining her to my side while we slept.

And maybe Allie needs this, too.

Because she fidgets again, but this time a soft moan accompanies the movement.

Silky wetness eases the journey from her clit to the small opening of her cunt, and I carefully circle the ring of softened flesh and groan. She's going to strangle my cock when I bury deep inside and stretch my innocent girl's tight little pussy.

I lick behind her ear, savoring the salty sweet taste of her skin as she writhes into my hand and cock, rubbing every beautiful curve against me, searching for satisfaction.

Grunting, I readjust behind her so my body has more leverage, practically dry humping her into the mattress with each heavy rock of my hips.

Fuck these damn clothes.

My sweatpants and her cotton shorts offer an annoying barrier when all I want is to slide between the deep valley of her ass cheeks while finger fucking her pussy.

Allie whimpers, and the sound goes straight to my balls. They're heavy and full and ready to shoot a steady stream of cum over my girl's pretty little body.

"*C'est ça, mon petit ange.* Come for me," I rasp, my harsh breaths filling her ear. "*Ton cul parfait est sur le point de me faire jouir. Tu es si belle, ma douce fille.*"

Our bodies shudder in near unison, first hers then mine, until I sink bonelessly into her, allowing my weight to anchor her to the bed.

"Wh... What just happened?"

Allison's groggy voice holds a note of panic, so I quickly shift to my side and roll her over to face me. It spreads the sticky mess we made on the sheets, but I don't care.

That's one of the perks of having a woman of my own—the convenience of wet pussy wrecking my cock and bed whenever I want it.

"You came for me like I commanded." I suck the glossy evidence of her orgasm from my fingers.

Damn, she tastes good.

"But..."

A fist bangs on the door, and Allie startles like that nervous little bunny again.

"Hey, lazy bones. Our security access was finally cleared for Petit Enterprises. When you're ready to grace us with your presence, we can start combing through their records to nail Louis," Luca calls out, amusement coating his tone.

Jackass.

Unless he checked next door first, he couldn't know for sure if Allie was in my bed, but it's not too much of a gamble to assume she is, which means he wanted to interrupt whatever we were doing.

Just like an annoying brother.

"That sounds important. I'm going to..." Allie tries to extricate herself from my embrace, but I stop her with a firm hand to her hip.

"Explain the details of your health," I finish her sentence.

"We went over this last night. There's not much more to tell."

"I disagree." Then I ask the questions raised from last night. Because there's no way in hell I'm letting her downplay anything.

At first, Allie hems and haws, trying to get away with vague answers, then she realizes I'm not letting her leave this bed until I get what I want.

She finally relents with an aggrieved sigh and draws the comforter up to her shoulders, staring at the ceiling as her story unfolds.

"Growing up, I dealt with what I'd now categorize as OCD, anxiety, and depression. I worried about making friends or saying the wrong thing in class. At home, my parents fought a lot, and I was their unofficial mediator. I made it my responsibility to save their marriage, to protect my little brother from their fights. All of it, school and my family, created an anxious perfectionist who was slowly dying inside," she admits.

"What you saw last night started in high school. I can't pinpoint the exact event that triggered it, but one day, I stared at a bottle of ibuprofen for too long, imagining what would happen if I swallowed every pill." Her voice takes on a far-off quality like she's drifted back to that time to relive the moment. "It made me feel a little better." She shrugs as best she can while laying down. "And I figured it was harmless since I didn't plan on actually following through with the thought."

A vulnerable teen Allison causes an unfamiliar pinch in my heart. I didn't have a great childhood either. Hugo's dad raised us as manipulative and dangerous mercenaries. I knew how to infiltrate a building and kill a man with his own tie before learning how to drive.

But at least I had my brothers.

It sounds like my girl didn't have a strong support system. Even with a sibling, she was too entrenched as a protective figure, making it impossible to lean on her brother when she needed help, too.

"When did the medication and therapy start?" I ask, drumming out a random pattern on her hip with my fingers.

Her nose scrunches up as she mentally calculates the time. "About four years ago? I tried therapy first, and while I liked my therapist, I didn't feel much improvement. Then my doctor suggested a combination solution, so I switched therapists, got on the meds, and that's where I am today. There was a lot of trial and error between different medications and doses until we landed on something that worked."

"But it's not one hundred percent foolproof."

A sigh of resignation warms my chest as she ducks her head. "No, though I'm not sure that's possible."

"Have you talked with your doctors about changing things since you're still experiencing..." I mull over the best way to define yesterday's episode, but Allison saves me from completing the thought.

"The problem doesn't lie with the meds or therapy. It's the situations I put myself in that exacerbate things. When I'm not in toxic environments, like living with Bailey or my family, I've never felt better. My issue is unknowingly falling back into those patterns. It's not like I would have agreed to room with Bailey if I knew I'd find myself in a similar mental space as I did with my parents."

"That won't happen again. I won't let it."

She laughs. "You can't guarantee that. Frankly, my past bad decisions are part of the reason I should go home. I never should have agreed to this arrangement. My only excuse for yesterday is that you caught me at a vulnerable time, but it was momentary. I'm better now."

"You literally had a blade to your wrist mere hours ago. You're not better now," I scoff in disbelief. The puzzle of Allison is slowly coming together, but she's still full of contradictions. Surprises.

"I mean this has been a wake-up call. You pushed me out of the apartment with Bailey, which I appreciate, but I can handle the rest from here. I'll go back to North Carolina and use the money you gave me for a hotel until I find a new place to live."

"No."

"What do you mean, *no*?" Allison wiggles to a sitting position and stares down at me, a frown wrinkling her face.

Matching her position, I rise up enough that our eyes are even. "There's not a chance in hell you're leaving. Not the state. Not Boston. Not this damn room if you insist on being difficult."

She sputters with indignation. A spark of fire I've been missing. That her family and friends attempted to snuff out.

"Excuse me? Being difficult? I'm letting you off the hook. Yesterday was a weird day. An anomaly. We're strangers who let emotions control our actions, but today will be different. You can return to focusing on the trouble with your dad, and I can rebuild the progress I made before everything went down with Bailey."

Allie can fight this all she wants, but she's not going anywhere. Not without my approval. I've got a contingent of Blackthorn men—ex-military, mostly—who will ensure she stays exactly where I want her.

Spying the time on the nightstand clock, I pat her hip again then get out of bed. Luca may be aggravating, but he's got a point about our need to go through Petit's records. It's already two hours past the time I'd normally start work, which is jarring.

I never sleep in.

I'm never late.

"Here's your first lesson about me: I don't let emotions control anything I do." Have they come close when Allie's in the picture? Perhaps. But I've reined them in and decided my next steps based on pure, hard logic.

Allison unwittingly offered the perfect antidote to cure the feral hunger I keep chained tightly within. I rule decisively and purposefully in everything I do, which requires a cool head. A calm demeanor.

Neither of those things comes easily when there's a part of me that yearns to break free and control situations.

Employees who make mistakes? I wish I could shake sense into them.

Peers who ignore my advice? I'd like to force them to listen and heed my words.

But that's not acceptable behavior in a businessman. In anyone really.

No one likes to be told what to do. Least of all me.

So, I tamp down the instinct that wants me to shout "I know what's best for you," breathe a sigh of relief when people's decisions work out, and bite my tongue when they don't.

Until Allison.

She gave me free rein over her life yesterday.

She agreed to let me take care of her and do what's in her best interest.

She did it gratefully. Willingly. Beautifully.

And I won't let her take it back.

That's the cold, hard, *logical* truth.

CHAPTER FIFTEEN

ALLISON

The grandfather clock in the corner of the library chimes ominously. *Once. Twice. Three times.* A vestige of the past, and an integral part of Blackchapel Manor's gothic atmosphere.

Despite the modern conveniences, an underlying hum of a bygone era emanates from the old brick and dark woods that characterize the manor.

If I wasn't so fixated on my current circumstances, I'd explore its many rooms and halls, eager to stumble upon secret passages and hidden alcoves.

One. Two. Three.

3:00 P.M.

Hours since I scurried from Mathias's bed to my own, then wandered around until I found this shelf-lined room. Camped out on a window seat, I've been staring at dormant garden hedges as if they hold the answers to my problems.

A stranger appeared on my doorstep and whisked me away to his den of danger. He fed me. Held me. And I reveled in his skilled touch this morning. Like we were more than a woman recovering from a near mental breakdown and a man who inexplicably chose to take her under his villainous wing.

"You don't know that he's a villain," I mumble to myself in the ensuing quiet, the sonorous signals of the time resting until the next hour.

Except he and his brothers are targets of an entire criminal organization.

One Mathias is determined to burn to the ground after being trained to kill.

"There you are. Someone is here to see you." Mathias strides into the library and offers his hand like a gentleman of old. From the tailored suit to his well-coiffed hair—strands of silver beginning to shine at the temples—a classic sort of charm limns his muscular form, belying the contemporary edge of danger that clings to him.

Reluctantly, I place my hand in his and follow him through a maze of corridors.

"I don't know anyone in Boston." Our footsteps are muffled by yards of carpet runners, yet I wonder if he heard me when there's no response.

We stop in front of my bedroom, and Mathias knocks once before opening the door. An older woman stands alert and waiting by the heavy oak dresser. A large leather bag hangs from her gathered hands.

"Hello, you must be Allison. I'm Dr. Bellamy."

Mathias gently pushes me forward when I stumble to a halt. "Dr. Bellamy is here for a health workup. She'll also be administering your birth control."

Birth control!

A million questions burst to life. How does he know I'm not already on something? Is this what he really wants from me? Sex? The idea seems laughable considering he's attractive and wealthy enough to not have to *import a woman from out of state* to warm his bed.

And why a complete health workup?

Because he found you with a razor to your wrist, heard about your issues, and questioned the wisdom of his decision to keep you.

"I'll be right across the hall if you need anything," he says, then shoots a withering glare at the doctor. "You came highly recommended, Dr. Bellamy. It'd be a shame to cut such an illustrious career short if you harm Miss Fields."

That growled warning should not be hot.

He just threatened the poor woman—a health professional who took an oath to literally do no harm. He's psycho, even while draped in cool lethality.

The door clicks shut, and Dr. Bellamy and I share a wary look of commiseration.

"Shall we begin?" She forces a timorous smile and unzips her bag, grabbing a stethoscope before motioning for me to sit on the end of the bed.

I obey her soft requests.

I don't make small talk.

And when it comes time for the birth control discussion, I opt for the shot. There's no way I'm adding another freaking pill to my regimen.

"You're all set." She snaps a pocket on her bag closed—my vials of blood safely stored within for lab testing. "I'll be back in twelve weeks for your next shot, but here's my card if you need to reach me beforehand."

A white rectangle with a local hospital address is placed in my hand, and I thank her. She's gone above and beyond. Big city doctors don't make house calls these days, and I know it's because Mathias intimidated her. Probably threatened to ruin her career again... or worse.

Once she's gone, Mathias reenters the room.

"How'd it go?" he asks, sitting so close beside me on the bed that his firm thigh warms my much softer one.

"Fine. She's nice. No need to ruin her life."

"Good to hear. My schedule's already pretty booked."

For a moment, I freeze, then an unexpected giggle surges from my throat. "Did you just make a joke?"

His hand lightly cups my neck over the vibrating sounds, and they immediately evaporate. "Don't stop," he murmurs. "I like your laugh, and that's the first time you've smiled since yesterday."

"Can you blame me?" My voice is low to match his. Like we're whispering secrets. Like I'm not vulnerable beneath his callused fingers. "My life isn't my own anymore."

"That was true long before you met me, *ma cherie*."

My shoulders slump at the matter-of-fact statement, and I unconsciously lean forward to feel the pressure of his large palm with every swallow.

My lashes flutter shut as a strange calm streams over doubts and fears like the ocean's tide coasting along dips of ever shifting sand.

"You're safe now. Free to smile and laugh as often as you want. If anyone tries to steal that away from you again, I'll break their fucking neck."

His hand reflexively tightens, but I'm not scared. Mathias won't hurt me. For better or worse, I trust him.

I'm safe.

I'm not alone.

CHAPTER SIXTEEN

ALLISON

"How long are we saying this is okay?" Rafe asks from his side of the couch in the game room.

Of the five Blackchapel Bastards I've met, he's the one I've seen the most outside of Mathias. Which is how he roped me into playing video games with him every afternoon while Mathias holed up in his home office with Luca, Hugo, and Jonah, poring over Petit Enterprises company files.

The details of what they're searching for are a bit vague, but that's probably for the best.

I don't need to get more wrapped up in Mathias's life than necessary since I'm sure he'll eventually get bored with this thing between us. I've seen enough of his life at the manor to know we're as different as humble apple pie and Michelin-starred truffles.

He grew up in this massive mansion full of expensive artwork, state-of-the-art security, and a no-nonsense housekeeper who manages the eight people who sweep in and out every day to clean and cook for the entire household.

I grew up in one small apartment after another, running from eviction notices, as my parents struggled to figure out the simple concept of not spending more money than you earn.

Sure, Mathias was also raised by an evil man bent on revenge, but a mom and dad bent on tearing each other apart and putting their kids in the middle leaves its own sort of trauma.

The point is Mathias travels on a level of society where the bar for moral integrity may be low but the bank accounts are high, and I'm just a regular girl who felt uncomfortable treating myself while in Paris.

Maybe that's why Mathias's brothers weren't exactly thrilled when they first met me.

They were friendly but wary, clearly confused about my connection to Mathias. And now that they've overheard me pleading my case to return home, it's obvious they're uneasy with the entire situation. Apparently, kidnapping doesn't sit well with a group of men raised to kill.

Who knew?

Granted, Mathias doesn't refer to getting me out of 'that hellhole' as kidnapping but *tomato/potato*, or something like that.

"We're not saying this is okay. Period." I slam my thumb on one of the controller buttons to send my race car surging forward. "Mathias is being stubborn, so it's a matter of waiting him out. He'll come to his senses eventually."

Rafe snorts. "You don't know Mathias."

I groan as his black car cuts me off on the huge television screen. "That's the point. Besides, I don't know what he expects me to do around here. I can't play video games with you all day."

"You have two million dollars in your bank account," a familiar voice calls. Mathias stands straight and tall in the doorway with a bottle of water in his hand. "Do something with it. Plus, you've got movies, games, a pool. Think of it as an extended vacation."

"One I have to take against my will."

He shrugs as if to say 'I don't know what to tell you' before changing the subject. "Did you eat lunch?"

"Yes, mother. She ate a chicken quesadilla with me before we started playing," Rafe interjects, rolling his eyes at Mathias's mother henning.

"Good." Mathias pins me with a look of approval that brings heat to my cheeks, sets the water in front of me, then stalks back to his office. One of his many check-ins officially completed.

As I turn back to the game, embarrassed by my immediate response to his one word of praise, I contemplate my future.

Am I willing to go back to North Carolina and start fresh? Yes, of course.

I've recovered from my minor breakdown, which honestly happened at least once a month with Bailey. It took that long for everything I bottled up to explode into a blubbering, hopeless mess. But now I've had my release, and I'm good to go.

Don't think about releases! The prudish voice of an old Sunday school teacher screeches in my head.

But it's already too late. The memory of Mathias's hard body grinding against mine, his thick fingers stroking me from the inside out. It sends more heat traveling lower to settle between my thighs as ghost sensations prickle along my skin.

Every morning, I wake to a mood boosting orgasm, thanks to his talented hands, and I can only imagine what his tongue or cock...

Ugh, no!

More unwelcome, *inconvenient* thoughts.

I refuse to let hormones cloud my judgment when I get enough of that with my imbalanced brain chemistry.

The point is I'm ready to forget my minor lapse of independence. I'm perfectly capable of handling my affairs by myself.

Mathias knows it.

His brothers know it.

There's just one tiny, troublesome problem I keep trying to ignore—the unfortunate truth that part of me wants to stay and live in this weird fantasy world for as long as Mathias lets me.

And how wrong is that?

How totally screwed up do you have to be to want something like that?

Then to actually be *thankful* for Mathias's stubbornness in not letting me go.

It plays into my dreams of someone fighting for me. Someone caring enough to want me around. Who won't be dissuaded by my half-hearted protests because they care too much for me.

Now, am I delusional enough to believe Mathias is on his way to falling in love with me? Ha! The possibility is so laughable I'm liable to turn into that scene from *Mary Poppins* where they laugh so hard they end up on the ceiling.

But he feels *something*, and it's strong enough to warrant him warning the security guards stationed outside the manor to not let me through the gates without his presence.

He happily notified me of *that* particular rule about an hour after dinner that first evening.

So, I'm torn between what I should do and what I want to do, which honestly is the story of my life, and why I've secretly yearned for someone to make the decisions for me in the first place.

You're going in circles now.

Because I'm right back to the beginning, rehashing the same thoughts over and over again.

"Hey, do you want to play another game?" Rafe asks. He's technically the youngest, but that hardly makes him boyish. He's just as muscular and hardened-looking as the other brothers but with a spark of humor that slightly lightens the dark shade of gray hanging over this place.

"What? Racing is fine. Why?"

"Because you seem distracted. If you're not interested in this, we can—"

"No, sorry. I'm good." *Just trying to spiral into another anxiety attack. No biggie.*

My phone dings, and I really don't want to check it. Since leaving North Carolina, my inbox has blown up with angry messages from Bailey as the movers Mathias hired gathered my stuff. And on top of her texts, my brother keeps hounding me for the money to pay his phone bill because an unexpected expense made him short this month.

Based on the photos he's shared on social media of multiple nights clubbing with friends, I can guess what his unexpected expenses were.

Preparing myself for either Bailey or Josh, I'm pleasantly surprised when it's neither. Then confused.

"That's odd."

"What? That someone's texting you?" Rafe jokes.

"No..." I lightly slap his arm. "It's the pharmacy letting me know that my prescription will be delivered tomorrow."

"Isn't that a good thing?"

"Not when I didn't submit a refill request or switch to a Boston pharmacy. I think I was hacked."

Rafe is quiet for a moment before he chuckles and bumps my shoulder with his. "Yeah, by Mathias. Or me, after Mathias asked me to transfer your prescriptions to a local store and set up auto delivery."

"He did what?" Shock zaps down my spine, and I consciously ignore the other reaction the news brings—unabashed pleasure at the forethought.

"I probably shouldn't tell you about your therapist either, huh?"

"Did something happen to Tasha?"

Rafe shrugs while shaking his head, keeping his focus on the game while I've completely abandoned it.

"She wouldn't have been able to continue being your therapist since she wasn't licensed in Massachusetts, but that's taken care of now. Her license is being expedited after some finagling to get her to apply."

My eyes widened. "You *spoke* to Tasha?"

"Not me. Mathias," he says. "Are you sensing a theme here? Mathias is the mastermind behind all of this. I'm just the tech guy tapping away on the computer."

I sink into the couch and watch as Rafe zooms around the track on the screen. It hadn't even occurred to me that I'd need to switch therapists.

And now, thanks to Mathias and Rafe, I apparently won't have to.

"How did he even know there was going to be an issue with her licensing?"

"One thing you'll learn about Mathias is that he's like the Eye of fucking Sauron, and we're just the orcs living under his rule of Mordor following his command."

"Speak for yourself, I'm a hobbit." I'd like to be an elf, but I'm nowhere near gorgeous or thin enough.

"Okay, fine. You're a hobbit, but unlike in the movie, Mathias *sees* you, and he's scary good at anticipating what people might need."

"That's comforting, especially since you're comparing him to a character villain."

"Babe, you didn't think we were the heroes did you?"

"Don't call her *babe*." Mathias's sharp voice rings from the doorway.

"Couldn't stay away, could you?" Rafe taunts.

"Just thought I'd give you some real competition." Mathias sits down and tugs me closer to him, adding space between me and his brother.

"I take offense to that. I'm getting pretty good at this game."

The two men share a look over my head, and I huff in mock annoyance. It's kind of nice being teased by them. Like I'm part of the family.

Too bad it won't last.

CHAPTER SEVENTEEN

MATHIAS

After spending the day studying Petit Enterprises files for more damning ammunition against my father, video games with Rafe and Allie are a welcome breather, while dinner with my brothers and my girl brings a sense of peace I've been missing.

But the best part of my day is when I'm free to coax Allie upstairs to our bedroom.

Not just mine anymore.

Ours.

Each morning, I've wakened with a raging need to fuck her, and each time, I've settled for humping her lush ass as I finger her pussy. It's my way of giving her time to adjust to the fact that she's mine and I intend to fuck her ten ways to Sunday as often as I can.

Never say I'm not a gentleman.

"I don't know how I can be so tired when I barely do anything during the day." Allie covers a yawn. "Rather than resigning for me, you should have convinced my job to let me work remotely. Then I'd have something to fill my time."

She'd been pissed when I told her about the email I'd sent to her former employer. Her cheeks had flushed and her mouth had formed a mutinous line, but that's as far as she allowed her anger. Her need to avoid confrontation curtailing the emotion. I hate that she's learned that's the best way to protect herself.

Allie shouldn't hide her feelings from anyone, least of all me. She deserves to freely express herself without fear of rejection or judgment.

"How about I give you a legitimate reason for exhaustion?" I ask, wicked intention coating the question. Perhaps it's time to push her boundaries a little bit more.

Wariness vibrates from her position by the bedroom window as I stalk forward. Her gaze flits to the bed then back to me.

"Mathias..."

My hands circle her waist. Soft. Supple. A body made for a man to sink into. For *me* to hold and worship and possibly find peace.

"Allie Angel..." I whisper the words over the rapid pulse in her neck. "Don't turn me away. Haven't I made you feel good every morning?"

"Yes, but—"

"Do you want me to take it? Is that what my girl needs?"

Her breath hitches, and I swear I can smell the sweet gush of arousal between her thighs.

The beast inside becomes feral.

Allie's a good girl.

But she yearns to be claimed and fucked without the niceties. Those *too good*, *too proper* chains prevent her from feeling comfortable enough to voice the need.

But I don't need verbal consent.

Allie's responsive body says all that's necessary.

"The safe word is *peppermint*. Repeat it back to me."

"P-Peppermint."

"Good girl." I spin her around and guide Allie to the mattress, pressing her down flat on her back with my body.

When we're both horizontal, I balance on my side so one hand can roam the malleable hills and valleys of her curves. "Tonight is about you, Allie Angel. I'm going to caress and kiss, and you're going to talk to me."

She jolts like a wire zapped with electricity. "About what? Why?"

Allie's always full of questions. Always needing the safety found in knowledge. It's a common trait we share.

"Because I like hearing your voice," I admit. Honeyed tones, rich and sweet, it's a welcome change from the rumble of males that usually fills the manor. "And because we're going to replace your negative thoughts and memories with positive ones. We're removing their power. Starting tonight."

"I don't understand..." Prudence wars with the desire in her eyes as I remove her glasses and toss them by the pillow.

"You will," I promise. "Why don't you tell me about the last time you considered hurting yourself, and we'll begin."

CHAPTER EIGHTEEN

ALLISON

We'll begin.

Mathias's warm palm glides down my chest to cup my breast. His touch is dulled by my shirt and bra, but not enough to stop the rush of arousal slicking my core.

"I'm waiting, *ma cherie.*"

He wants me to spill my dark thoughts. Lance the puffy abscesses as if his touch will miraculously cure me of their infectious claws.

It's a ridiculous notion, yet words spill out of me anyway. Slow and stuttering before building momentum.

"The night I got home from Paris, I was exhausted from the flight and the antibiotics for the bullet wounds. All I wanted to do was fall into bed and sleep for the next forty-eight hours."

His breath coasts over my neck while he massages my breast, toying with the nipple. The scratch of his beard tickles. His lips tease.

And I continue.

"Bailey called at midnight. It's a miracle I even woke up." My mind flashes back to the memory, and an anxious itch rakes over my skin before I'm distracted by the rasp of Mathias's tongue on my inner elbow.

When did he get there?

"I'm not sure what she was doing out, but she got in a car accident. No one was hurt, but her car was totaled, and she needed a ride." The crushing desire to refuse her had reared up, but I'd stamped it out.

I couldn't leave her stranded.

I couldn't abandon her.

"I drove to get Bailey. Waited in my car for another hour and a half because she didn't tell me she hadn't dealt with the tow truck and cops yet."

That's when the numbness really set in. I remember wishing I could rest. Wondering what Bailey would have done if I didn't exist. If I wasn't around to help her.

Mathias's mouth skims my belly underneath the cotton tee. He wrangles my black leggings and panties down my legs then kisses the stretch marks on my thighs.

What was I saying?

"Go on, baby. Tell me what happened next." He nuzzles between my thighs, breathing in and out, a muted groan rolling over my sensitized flesh.

His tongue burrows through the folds to lap at my clit, and I whimper at the unfamiliar sensation.

My sexual experience is fairly limited—my last relationship ended four years ago, and we never went *all the way*. I was waiting for a deeper commitment before losing my virginity, and he thought oral sex was unsanitary. Unnecessary.

Judging by the sloppy sounds of bliss coming from Mathias, he disagrees.

"Bailey was pissed about her car. She didn't thank me for picking her up." I fight to speak coherently through spikes of pleasure. I'm not sure if Mathias's unconventional therapy has merit, but I'm definitely feeling something other than the despair of that night.

"When I got home, I stared at my pill organizer. That pink cylinder with the glitter?" I reference the container he's seen me pull out every morning before breakfast. "I'd just refilled compartments. Hundreds of pills. And I wondered what it'd be like to swallow them all."

A hard suck on my clit slaps the desperate musing aside. Two long fingers plunge into my soaking channel. "Your worthless roommate got off easy," he growls between nips and sucks. "If I ever see—"

"Stop." My hands tangle in his short hair, tugging on the silver-streaked strands. "I don't want to think about her anymore. I just want to feel. You're the only one who makes me *feel*," I admit, arching into his ravenous mouth.

Mathias cracks the layer of numbness between me and the world. He's done it from the moment we first met. Effortlessly. Assertively. It's why I keep pushing to leave here.

Glimmers of myself sprout through those cracks, and the independent woman who is used to being responsible and taking care of herself can't resist vying for control again.

Another lick. Another finger added to stretch my tight opening. And Mathias wins, ushering in a blinding orgasm that obliterates thoughts of Bailey, suicide, and self-doubt.

I relish his attention. His thumb circling my throbbing clit as he kisses back up my body. His bearded cheek scraping along mine.

It's a testament to how touch-starved—*affection-starved*—I am that we're both still mostly clothed, yet I feel as vulnerable and exposed as if I were lying naked before him.

When my vision clears enough to see his handsome face hovering above mine, the gleaming sight of my arousal on his lips and beard has me squirming in place.

It's raw and sexy and... *tastes like us*.

Mathias drops his head to claim my mouth in a possessive kiss, his tongue a mix of me and his unique flavor, and I realize this is our first kiss. He's fucked me with his fingers, and now his tongue, but he's never kissed me on the mouth before.

As if sharing the same thought, displeasure rumbles from his chest. "*Je suis désolé, mon ange.* You deserve to be kissed morning, noon, and night, and I plan on making up for my error."

Heart melting under his embrace, I stroke his scalp, his neck, his broad shoulders—anywhere I can reach—and enjoy the grounding effect his hard body has on mine.

No matter how wrong it may be, I could become used to being pinned beneath Mathias while he kisses my worries away.

CHAPTER NINETEEN

ALLISON

But kisses can only keep worries away for so long, and the numbness seeps forward again as the days pass with little fanfare.

Mathias and his brothers jet from the study to the security room to a large area converted into conference space for Blackthorn meetings. All very routine and boring, considering their ruthless reputations.

While I do nothing.

I don't have a job anymore. My time isn't monopolized by staying afloat while Bailey and my family try to drown me with their problems.

I need a purpose.

Who am I without the manacles of others clasped around me?

While ambling through the Blackchapel gardens, I've been asking myself that question for the last quarter of an hour with little to show for it. Except for my love of musicals as the question follows the tune of Jean Valjean's decree in *Les Miserables*.

Who am I?

If only it were as easy as shouting, "24601!"

The crunch of gravel interrupts my musings, then the familiar rasp of Mathias's voice snaps the quiet solitude.

"I've been looking for you."

Pausing my journey through the dormant rose bushes, I shrug, keeping my back to him. "Here I am. Do you need something? Figured you'd be locked inside for another hour or two."

"I needed a break and wanted to see you. Petit's records were beginning to give me a headache." His hand reaches for mine. "Where are your gloves? You're freezing."

"I'm fine." I pull free, a chill chasing his brief warmth away, but the weather isn't to blame for my numbness. "The garden will bloom soon. It's hard to believe spring is so close."

"It's not here yet," he says, recapturing my fingers before they trail over another empty stem of thorns. "Is something wrong? You were subdued at lunch, and now you're wandering outside like a ghost."

A half-hearted "Boo!" tumbles free at the comparison. Glancing back at the manor, the imposing brick stands stalwart in the late afternoon light, a web of vines forming nature's armor. The window to our room reflects the sun. Shunning its bright rays. The perfect home for a lost spirit.

Is something wrong?

Where should I begin?

"What am I doing here, Mathias?"

His jaw clenches, and the lines around his silver eyes deepen. "What do you mean? You're here to live free of the people who have mistreated you for years."

A bitter laugh bubbles up. "That's all well and good, except it's not a true answer. It's not a future. There's nothing for me to do here. I can't while away the rest of my life haunting this manor. I need more."

And god, do I feel greedy voicing the desire. Why isn't it enough that I'm safe and never need to worry about money again?

Maybe spending so much time with Mathias and his brothers—men who have a true purpose—has rubbed off on me.

Or maybe lazing around the manor reminds me too much of Bailey, and I don't want to be anything like her.

Mathias studies my desperate expression, a calculated look transforming his features. Stepping closer, he recaptures my hand and gently breathes a stream of warm air over my chilled skin.

"Why don't I take you to Polina's Place?" he asks with cautious optimism. "It's a safe house for women and children of domestic violence. One that's funded by Dmitri and Aleksei. You can meet the house manager, Jessie, and discuss volunteer opportunities. Or she can share what it's like running a non-profit organization if you think you'd like to start one."

"Start one?" The suggestion is so out of the blue I almost laugh again, but based on his sober visage, he's serious.

Mathias guides our steps back to the manor. "How many times have I said that you can do anything you want? You have two million dollars and more if you need it." He stops long enough to cup my icy cheek. He was right earlier; I *am* freezing.

"I know you've never had the luxury of time or money to discover what it is you need versus what everyone else requires. You've been getting by, surviving, but that's over now, Allie. You have options. Freedom. Use it."

Freedom.

Options.

Isn't that what I've always wanted?

But choice comes with risks. For so long, I've been pummeled by the waves of life. Fighting to stay above water as one problem after another battered my flailing limbs.

Life has happened *to* me.

I've rarely taken the opportunity to influence it. To be an active participant. That's the consequence of allowing other people to command my attention. For focusing on helping them improve their lives versus prioritizing mine.

Maybe Mathias's suggestion won't be the right fit. Or maybe it'll inspire me in a certain direction. But I won't know until I make a decision.

Until I take another step forward and start living life on my own terms.

"I'd like to see Polina's Place, if it's not too much trouble," I say. The caveat softens my assertion, but it's still a win. A move in the right direction.

One more step.

***

Two hours later, Mathias leaves me with Jessie, a peppy young woman, who outlines how Polina's Place runs.

"We're equipped to care for fifteen women and children at this location, but there's a larger apartment-type building downtown where we can take in more. This home is for those that need a little extra care and distance from crowds." She waves a hand to encapsulate the stately Victorian home on several acres of land.

A world away from the bustling city, it's easy to see why this little slice of heaven would feel safer for the most vulnerable residents.

"Mathias said you'd like to volunteer. What sort of talents do you have? We try to match tasks to volunteer strengths."

Shit. My day job skills are the only things I can think to offer, my mind totally blanking on what talents I possess. I'm not a hobbyist who gathers a variety of expertise in her spare time. I'm a homebody who reads or binges TV to escape reality.

If they need someone to watch *The Mentalist* and swoon over Simon Baker with, then I'm their girl. Otherwise? I feel pretty useless.

"I'm a graphic designer. My job was to handle the marketing materials for my last company."

"Excellent!" Jessie claps her hands in excitement as our tour comes to an end at the front of the house.

Mathias waits on the wraparound porch with the head of our security detail, Nathaniel. He's the stoic type—quiet and alert, always searching for danger.

"Why don't we go to my office, and we can discuss what's coming up event-wise and have you work your magic?"

"I can't guarantee magic," I joke, "But I'm happy to do whatever I can."

My natural tendencies lead me to help others, and Polina's Place is full of women and children who deserve it. They're not selfish or greedy. They don't want to use me rather than put in the work themselves like Bailey or my family.

They won't distort my instinct to help into its most toxic form. This is a good place.

A good first step to figuring out who I want to be.

A good first step toward building a life in Boston... *with Mathias.*

CHAPTER TWENTY

MATHIAS

LUCA: *Come to the chapel. There's someone here you'll want to meet.*

The text interrupts hours of combing through lines of black and white data, so I'm happy for the reprieve.

ME: *Be there in a sec.*

Stretching my arms overhead, I check on Allie in the corner of the study, where she's clicking away on her new laptop, working on the fundraiser brochures she promised Jessie for Polina's Place.

I'm glad our visit to Dmitri and Aleksei's non-profit inspired Allie. Anything that makes her smile, while also planting roots in Boston, is a win in my book.

"I've got to meet Luca at the chapel. Is there anything you need before I leave?" I ask, bracing a hand on her shoulder and bending to press a kiss to the top of her head.

I like having her here with me.

These past few days have been filled with comfortable companionship as we concentrated on our separate projects, and there's something to be said for having a beautiful woman close by when it's time for a break.

"No, I'm good." Allie barely lifts her head as she shifts a paragraph of text across the screen.

"Alright. I'll be back soon." Noting the time on my watch, I detour to the kitchen on my way to the chapel and ask Mrs. Shandy to drop off a snack for my hardworking girl, before resuming the short trek outside.

Years have passed since my brothers and I were expected to attend lessons in the crumbling chapel, but we still use it for the nastier side of Blackthorn.

Because what's more blood seeping into the stained stones? They can't get any more tainted. Can't tell the stories of the men who died here.

Speaking of which...

The first thing I see upon entering the chapel is a man tied to a chair at the cracked altar.

"Look familiar?" Luca asks from his lounging position on an old pew. "This man wielded the gun that shot your woman. Meet Richie Castellano."

Richie's eye is swollen shut and blood drips from a split lip, but he's not too fucked-up yet to be unrecognizable. Though he doesn't look as confident as he did hanging out of that van with a gun attached to his arm.

Luca cracks his knuckles, evidence of the punches our captive received written on the reddened skin, and silently nods toward Rafe, who stands with Hugo, Jonah, and Dmitri. The Blackchapel Bastards united for a shared cause—extracting information before exterminating the threat.

"Good work." I near the soon-to-be-dead man pissing himself in our chapel. Grabbing a patch of sweat-drenched hair, I yank his head back. "You made a grave mistake coming after us. The only question now is how you'll make up for it. Will you give us what we want in exchange for a quick death, or will you drag this out in a show of misguided loyalty?"

"Please... You've got the wrong man... I don't—"

With one powerful jab, my fist crunches through bone and cartilage to stop his blubbering, but then it's his howling cry over a broken nose that irritates my eardrums next.

"Christ!" I wince at the yowls bouncing off the stone walls. Removing a handkerchief from my suit pocket, I scrub Richie's blood away and nod toward Dmitri. "The second option, then."

As the head of Blackthorn, Dmitri is an expert at making people talk. We all have the skills, but it's his specialty. He's capable of keeping a prisoner alive for hours, chipping away at their body and psyche until they break.

It's a marvel.

And a long fucking way to spend the next few hours.

A grimace flattens my lips after another glance at my watch. I'd hoped to return to Allie rather than being stuck dealing with this pissant.

Is it too much to ask for a mafia grunt to spill his guts in exchange for a nice and easy snap of the neck?

Sighing, I roll my shoulders and join Luca on the pew. Sometimes being a Blackchapel Bastard really sucks.

***

"An acquaintance from Mass News emailed to let me know that an investigative journalist is writing an exposé on my dad," Jonah says around a bite of pizza. "Her name is Valerie Hale."

Once the mess in the chapel was dealt with, we agreed to a casual meal in the game room and a racing tournament to erase the tension of the day. Allie is firmly positioned on my lap as we devour slices of pepperoni pizza for dinner, and I can't help a swell of smug superiority.

My poor brothers don't get the benefit of a soft woman cozied up in their arms. They don't get to hear her quiet sounds of pleasure from the simple act of feeding her.

Only I get to experience those things.

Only I get to experience Allie.

And damn it feels good.

"Let's set up a meeting. She might be a useful contact to have in the future if she's capable of digging up dirt on politicians. It shouldn't be too difficult to do the same for a CEO or two."

I don't like bringing strangers into our business, but widening our network of resources is smart. Journalists usually have a list of confidential informants at their disposal.

Plus, the woman might have cultivated relationships out of our reach due to the indisputable fact that we can be damn intimidating.

Which sparks another idea.

"You should come with us." I gently jostle Allison.

"What?"

"I don't think that's a good idea."

I raise a hand to ward off the dissenting opinions. "We're the Blackchapel Bastards. If Valerie does even a minor internet search into us, it won't exactly inspire a sense of comfort. Having Allie there might change that and make her willing to share more information."

Jonah huffs then starts typing out a response on his phone. "I'll ask for her details."

"I still haven't agreed to go," Allie grumbles. Popping the last bite of crust in her mouth, she wipes her fingers on a napkin then asks Jonah, "Who's your dad?"

She knows the basics about Louis Petit, Enzo D'Amora, and Conrad Steele because of the drive-by and our training, but the rest of our fathers are mysteries.

"Senator Phillip Anderson."

"Damn..."

That about sums it up.

All of our fathers hold power one way or another outside The Syndicate. Which means, if we want to defeat them, our plans must be meticulous.

So I make damn sure they are.

CHAPTER TWENTY-ONE

ALLISON

The men decided it'd be safer to split up and take separate vehicles to the lunch spot for our meeting with the investigative journalist. Hugo and Luca are in a black Suburban ahead of us, while Jonah follows in a pickup truck. That leaves Mathias and I alone in his silver Audi.

"How did you know Tasha wouldn't be able to continue as my therapist without being licensed in Massachusetts?" I ask from the passenger seat. Since learning of his behind-the-scenes machinations, my curiosity has grown.

I managed to curb my questions because he's been busy compiling information on his dad, and I've been focused on volunteering at Polina's Place. *And enjoying the many Mathias-provided orgasms.*

The right time for discussing my therapist never appeared, but now we have time to kill, and I'm desperate to get answers. Especially since Tasha and I have a virtual appointment set for tomorrow morning.

"The medical records Rafe sent listed her licenses and qualifications. When I saw the state mentioned, it made me wonder if therapists worked under similar rules as lawyers where you have to be certified in whatever state you want to practice in," he explains, flipping on the turn signal to change lanes.

"From there, it was a simple phone call to Dr. Gomez. She tried to dismiss me with a bunch of patient-doctor confidentiality bullshit, but once I impressed upon her the importance of continuing her therapeutic relationship with you—*that it was in her patient's best interests*—she agreed to apply for a license to practice in Massachusetts. Usually it takes four to six weeks to finalize, but Rafe pushed it through much sooner."

"You have a copy of my medical records?" I swear the man has no boundaries.

What was your first clue? When he hacked into your bank account? Or when he commandeered a doctor for a home visit?

At least those results came back without any problems. Another health issue would have been the last straw.

My thirteenth reason, I privately joke.

Suicide isn't funny, but if my feelings don't allow for dark humor, then I'd really be screwed. Because sometimes a girl's just got to laugh at her fucked-up brain chemistry.

Historic brownstones pass along my right as we continue driving toward the coffee shop where our meeting is taking place. It's in downtown Boston and near the Mass News headquarters to make it an easy commute for Valerie.

The manor is about forty minutes outside the heart of the city, and with the change of scenery, it seems we're almost to our destination.

"Of course. I need to know your history, especially if I'm going to advocate for you."

Well, when he puts it like that...

Mathias has the uncanny ability to make an invasion of privacy seem like an act of protection, and it really fucks with my head. Because all I've ever wanted is to feel safe and secure.

Wanted.

Not alone.

I bang my head against the seat's headrest and groan. "For someone who scared the hell out of me in Paris, you're nothing like I expected."

"Don't think I'm not that man just because I'm excellent at keeping my promises. Like the one I made to care for you," he says, parallel parking on the street. "I'm still dangerous to be around. Just not for you."

Mathias winks, and it's so unexpected from his usually stoic expression that I sit stunned for a minute. Long enough for him to round the car, open my door, and unbuckle my seatbelt. "Come on. We've got ten minutes to walk a block to meet Valerie. There'll even be a hot caramel macchiato waiting for you when we arrive."

Because of course he ordered my favorite drink ahead of time.

The coffee shop bustles with locals grabbing their afternoon pick-me-up. Mathias and I skip the line and find our two drinks waiting on the front counter before heading back outside where Jonah procured a table on the sidewalk.

It's a little chilly for an outdoor meet-up, but the guys preferred the option of multiple exits rather than being surrounded by four walls. And who was I to argue with their tactical training?

"Relax," Mathias murmurs in my ear, holding out a metal chair for me to sit in.

I lower my bunched shoulders and try for an outwardly calm demeanor. This is my first foray into his world, and it feels a little too close to *The Sopranos* right now.

Mathias slings an arm over my shoulders like we're a normal couple out for coffee with a friend. Jonah sits across the table. Hugo and Luca remain hidden somewhere on the street to keep tabs on us in case something goes wrong, while Rafe monitors everything from the manor.

The other two Blackchapel Bastards, the brothers Dmitri and Aleksei, are busy, I guess—since one runs Blackthorn and the other is undercover in prison.

A young woman dressed in slacks and a fashionable blazer approaches our table, and I admire the business chic look she's got going on. I've seen videos of plus-sized fashion influencers showing off different outfits—my favorite is a woman named Nora who lives in a cute little mountain town called Suitor's Crossing—but this is the first time I've seen someone in the wild rock such a trendy look. It puts my basic sweater and jeans to shame.

"Hi, I'm Valerie Hale with Mass News." She offers a manicured hand to me and Mathias then turns to Jonah, her movement faltering before she quickly recovers. "Thank you for reaching out. I had no idea Senator Anderson has an illegitimate son. He hides you very well."

"Can't blemish his perfect political record," Jonah quips. His gaze hasn't left Valerie from the moment she arrived, and I wonder if this is another instance of a Blackchapel Bastard questioning a woman's willingness to help him.

Like Mathias did with me.

"He'll need to get over that, considering perfection is the opposite of how I'd describe his tenure with the government," Valerie says, occupying the last free chair at our table. She rests her leather tote in her lap while extracting a manila folder from its interior. "I hope that doesn't bother you. That I'll be reporting the truth about your father. It's not pretty."

Jonah and Mathias share a look then break into grins. "Anderson's dirty dealings are hardly news to us, which is why we asked for this meeting. We'd like to hear what you've learned and potentially offer our help. There's also the chance of another story that might interest you."

"Oh?" Valerie's brow raises as she sets the folder down and lowers the tote to the ground. Positioning her phone near the small centerpiece of fake flowers on the table, she asks, "Do you mind if I record our conversation? I promise it'll be kept between us."

The men nod, and one pink-tipped finger taps a button on the screen before Valerie launches into the details of her article, stunning me with how thorough her research is.

When I was in middle school, I toyed with the idea of becoming a journalist. There were always episodes in my favorite shows that featured a newspaper editor doling out interesting article ideas, while the writers got special privileges like going backstage at a concert to write a press release.

It seemed like an exciting job until I realized how much talking to strangers it involved. That's when I set that dream aside and forgot about becoming the next Barbara Walters.

But Valerie provides insight into the path not taken. I could've been the sexy sleuth penning a hard-hitting exposé about political corruption if I'd been braver.

Mathias's concern over Valerie feeling uncomfortable with the two men was probably unfounded. I can't imagine anything intimidating a woman willing to expose a prominent senator's wrongdoing. That's dangerous business in and of itself.

Which is why it shouldn't be a surprise when a single gunshot rings out, shattering the vase of flowers on our table.

"Get down!" Mathias shouts. His arm circles my shoulders as he drags me out of the chair and into his chest, both of us hunched over as he leads us to safety.

Another shot blasts through the air, causing PTSD to flare to life. I went my whole life never experiencing true danger. I dealt with emotional neglect and mental turmoil, but my parents never physically abused me. Now, I've been in the line of bullets twice.

Thanks to the Blackchapel Bastard determined to keep me.

Thanks to Mathias Beaumont.

CHAPTER TWENTY-TWO

JONAH ANDERSON

Chaos ensues after the gunshot. Coffee shop patrons scream, while Luca yells into my earpiece, letting Mathias and I know that he and Hugo are searching for the gunman.

Instinctively, my hand grabs Valerie's, and we race toward a large service van parked a few doors down. The vehicle's wide berth should provide enough protection from another bullet, but I'm fucking pissed at how close the first shot came to killing Valerie.

Based on the trajectory of that bullet, she was the target. Not me or Mathias or even Allison.

"Who else knows about your digging into Anderson?" I demand, casting a narrow gaze over the surrounding buildings, searching for clues as to who fired that shot.

"My editor. A couple of coworkers who were in the meeting when I pitched the idea to him." Valerie swallows hard and clings to the leather bag clutched between her white knuckles. "You think someone tried to hurt me?"

"Someone tried to *kill* you," I correct. "Injuring you won't stop your article from going to print. Once you recovered, you could start investigating again. This was meant to end the threat of exposure permanently."

She pales at the explanation.

"Oh my god. We need to go to the police. Let them know..."

"What? That a mystery shooter tried to take you out? We don't have proof they're connected to Anderson or you. The cops can write it off as a random act of violence, especially without an actual person in custody."

"But..."

"Trust me, the cops can't help you." *But I can.* I'll reassign a security team from Blackthorn to watch over her.

"Jonah, we think the shooter's gone. Hugo found his likely hiding spot. There was a cigarette butt left behind with a shell casing. Fucking amateur," Luca scoffs in my ear.

The assailant may not be a high-caliber professional, but his mediocre skills got him too close for comfort.

"Even an amateur's bullet can kill," I remind him. "I've got Valerie. How are Mathias and Allison?"

"Safe." Mathias's commanding tone enters the conversation. "Hugo, collect evidence from the site. Maybe we can track down a DNA match or fingerprint off them. Jonah, get Valerie to safety then meet us back at the manor."

"On it," Hugo says before signing off.

"Copy that. See you soon."

With the coast clear, I help Valerie unfold from her crouched position and guide her back onto the sidewalk. Police cars have set up a barricade in front of the coffee shop, and a couple of uniforms are cordoning off the space while a man and woman question café employees.

"It's safe now. The shooter is long gone."

"Because your backup says so?" She points to her ear, deducing that I'm wearing a comms piece after hearing me talking to myself.

"Yep. I'll walk you to your office building, but you'll need to be more careful going forward. Be aware of your surroundings." Because it's going to take a little time to organize a team I trust to watch her.

"I can handle myself, but thank you. I'll let you guys know if I find anything else out about your dad, and in the meantime, you have my email address and phone number. Give me a call if you learn something I can add to the article."

Grunting in agreement, I herd her closer to the buildings we pass, keeping my body between her and the street on our way to Mass News.

The steel and glass architecture gleams under the bright sun, blinding in its brilliance. A revolving door allows guests to enter and leave at will, and Valerie extends a hurried farewell before hightailing it toward the entrance.

She's tall for a woman. With thick curves perfectly outlined in her tailored outfit. She handled meeting Mathias and I—two of the notorious Blackchapel Bastards—with aplomb and didn't freak out once bullets started flying.

I like a woman who can keep her cool. I like her even better when she's determined to reveal my father for the corrupt politician he is, too.

Fuck it.

Before Valerie steps out of reach, I snake my arm around her wide hips and use her momentum to swing her back to me. Slamming my mouth down on her cherry red lips. Too tempted to sample the fire and sass within her prettily curved package.

And in the middle of the damn sidewalk, too.

Now isn't the time to be distracted by a woman, but what's one kiss?

A devil's kiss.
Because that's what I'd be for her.

CHAPTER TWENTY-THREE

MATHIAS

The car remains silent as I navigate the streets of Boston on our way home after the shitshow at the coffee shop.

I fucked up today.

As the leader, it's my job to ensure everyone's safety. I'm the 'paranoid' one. I consider potential threats and prepare for them.

So why wasn't there a contingent of Blackthorn soldiers surrounding the coffee shop? Why did I let that shooter get close enough to kill us?

It's unacceptable.

And I'm to blame.

If Allie had been hurt—*again*—because of me...

My fingers flex on the steering wheel.

I'm so damn tired of bullets and guns and assholes trying to kill me or my family. That's why my brothers and I are so determined to wipe The Syndicate off the face of the earth. Its disappearance won't eradicate every threat to our lives, but it will eliminate at least eighty percent of them.

Leaving a twenty percent that should be far easier to defend against.

Allie's phone vibrates for the fifth time in a row since she quietly buckled into the passenger seat. I keep stealing glances at her, worried today's events might send her into another anxiety attack, but she seems outwardly fine. Just contemplative.

Except for the sigh that follows a hastily typed message.

"Who's texting so much?" I ask.

Allie bites her lip in answer, physically holding back a reply. *As if I'll let her hide anything from me.* Every facet of Allie's life is important to me, because if I'm left in the dark on something, then I can't care for her properly.

"Allison..."

"It's Bailey, okay?"

"She's still bothering you after my warning?" The bitch must have a death wish. I made myself perfectly fucking clear. *Leave Allison alone.* "Give me your phone."

"What? Why? I'm handling this." She stretches to keep the device out of reach as if my arm span isn't longer than hers. We may be driving on a busy road, but I'm an excellent multitasker, and I always get what I want.

"If you were handling Bailey, then her number would already be blocked."

"I did at first. But then I got so anxious about something bad happening to her and not being able to reach me. It felt worse than dealing with her messages, so I unblocked her."

"Give me your phone, Allie." My hand rests on her warm thigh, palm up. She's got ten seconds to hand it over before I pull onto a side street and take it forcefully.

"You blocking her isn't going to make a difference." Her body becomes a rigid line of angles as she twists away from me.

"That's not what I'm doing. We're going phone shopping, so you won't need that dinosaur anymore."

"Wait, what?" Surprise has her muscles loosening a fraction.

"You're getting a new number, so Bailey can't contact you anymore. Besides, how old is that thing?" I gesture to the phone clenched in her hand.

"Three years old."

"Damn, baby, that's fucking ancient in technology."

She shakes her head defensively. "If it still works, then there's no reason to replace it for a higher definition camera or whatever."

"Oh, we're replacing it, but if it makes you feel better, we'll ask them to add your old phone to whatever recycling program they have. Now, I'm running out of patience. Are you going to give me your phone, or do you want to test me further?"

A strained minute passes before she reluctantly drops the phone in my hand.

"Thank you," I murmur, tucking the device into my coat pocket then capturing her free hand with mine.

It's a short drive to the store, and an associate welcomes us the moment we step foot inside.

I present Allie's antiquated phone to the man and explain the situation. "Transfer everything over except for the contacts."

By her own admission, Allison doesn't have a good support system, which means the only numbers she needs to keep are mine and my brothers in case of an emergency. Everyone else can fuck off.

They weren't there for my girl when she needed them, so they're out of her life.

No excuses.

I expect a fight about the contacts thing, but Allie remains silent. Whether it's because she doesn't want to cause a scene or not, I accept her hushed acquiescence. It makes this easier.

"Do you know what kind of phone you want to upgrade to?" Zayden the associate asks.

"Same as this one." I show him my device. When we get back to the manor, Rafe can add our special security apps to Allison's.

The man nods before setting the old phone on the counter and retreating to the back of the store for a new one. While he's gone, a text lights up the screen, and automatically, I go to answer it.

Bailey is done fucking with Allie.

But when I open the message, it's not from a disgruntled roommate, it's from Allie's brother, Josh.

There's a slew of texts from him.

First asking for help to pay his phone bill, then trying to guilt trip her when she refused. They coincide with another message that pops up leading to a conversation with their parents as her mom and dad pile on more guilt in an effort to make her help the family.

And I had no fucking idea this was going on.

"Why the hell didn't you tell me about this bullshit with your family?" Accusation vibrates throughout my body, along with derision for myself.

For a man who got his secret desire fulfilled with Allie, I'm doing a shit job at earning the privilege of calling her mine. She's still trying to deal with these stressors alone when I want her to give them to me.

I need to figure out a new game plan for gaining her trust.

Sure, she capitulated easily enough at her apartment, but since then, she's reverted back to being self-sufficient Allison Fields, and I've let her, to an extent, because I want her comfortable with me and the changes in her life. Especially after catching her that first night in the bathroom with a blade to her wrist.

Clearly, that was the wrong decision.

My girl needs a stronger hand.

Allie flushes bright red. "Because it doesn't concern you."

"The hell it doesn't."

Zayden returns before I can say much more, but my mind swirls with next steps.

Allison's grace period is over. She doesn't understand what it means for me to take care of her. She's still trying to do it herself as if nothing has changed except her location.

When we get back to Blackchapel Manor, she'll learn the truth. Except my plans are derailed by Luca as soon as we enter the manor foyer.

"Hey, do you have a second?" he asks, shooting Allie a small smile in greeting before gesturing toward the shared study.

I debate stalling him, but that would only be a temporary delay before he interrupts us again.

"Sure. I'll find you later, *cherie*." I watch her head upstairs, enjoying the view of her ass bouncing with each step, then follow Luca to the study. "What's up?"

"I'm wondering if we're still working on our original timeline for screwing over Petit."

"Of course we are. Nothing's changed."

"Except something has, and her name is Allison," Luca says pointedly. "Look, it was a surprise when you installed her in the manor, but we supported you, and we still do, even if we don't quite understand your plan. But you can't deny that you've been distracted. The deal on Petit Enterprises closed a while ago, yet you haven't mentioned going ahead with our next move, which is unlike you."

My brows furrow as frustration wells in my chest. I don't like being taken to task. No one berates my behavior and gets away with it. Not even my brothers.

"What do you call working with you and Jonah every damn day combing through Petit's records? We haven't compiled enough evidence to make a concrete case against him. That's not distraction or shortsightedness. It's called being fucking prepared."

Luca shakes his head. "Before Allison arrived, you wouldn't have stopped researching for *anything*. I've lost count of how many late nights we've shared because you wouldn't let any of us rest until we found whatever we were looking for. Now, we're heeding a routine schedule like nine to five grunts? Tell me that's not like you," he pushes.

"I'm going to say this once, then you're going to drop the subject, and you can let the rest of the guys know not to bring it up either. I haven't gone soft or stupid. Louis Petit will be dealt with soon; his assets drained so The Syndicate takes a massive hit. He's *my* father, and I want my revenge against him more than anyone in this damn house. Don't fucking forget it."

My fist pounds on the top of a leather armchair with a thump. Storming out of the room, I stomp up the stairs. Pissed doesn't begin to describe the war raging inside my veins.

Luca's wrong.

I'm in control of my feelings.

I'm hyper-focused on ruining Petit.

Allison hasn't changed those facts, because I refuse to let her. *I am in fucking control.*

CHAPTER TWENTY-FOUR

ALLISON

Mathias's conversation with Luca must not have gone well because the moment he stalks inside the bedroom, my guard rises.

I'm already on edge after the assassination attempt on Valerie, then fielding the barrage of texts from my family before Mathias confiscated my phone and replaced it.

I thought I'd have more than five minutes to gather myself before facing him again.

His movements are calm as he shoulders off his jacket and rolls up the sleeves of his buttoned shirt, but there's an underlying tension radiating through each snap of his fingers.

"I've done you a disservice, *mon petit ange*." The French endearment rolls off his tongue, dark and titillating. "I told you how things would be from now on. I've even given you glimpses of my intentions. But they haven't been enough. It's time I make sure you understand exactly what I want from you."

"Mathias..."

I shuffle away from him toward the walk-in closet. Perhaps with some distance, and a door between us, he'll calm down before doing whatever he's up to. Adrenaline pumps through my veins—fight or flight—as fear and arousal twine together in a twisted combination.

My hand grazes the closet's door handle, preparing to slam it shut, when Mathias swiftly strides forward and traps me against the island centered in the large space.

"A door won't save you." He lifts me onto the cold marble, and I shiver at the contact through my jeans.

I'm not afraid of Mathias. That would be too simple. Instead, my wariness is mixed with lust and anticipation and curiosity.

A potent elixir.

A dangerous one.

"You said you wanted me to shoulder your burdens for you, and I willingly accepted the responsibility." With each word, he removes a piece of my clothing.

Knit sweater. Jeans. Socks.

"You told me you were stuck, yet I haven't done my job of freeing you."

My bra loosens, and a tremulous breath follows.

Mathias touched me that first morning here—after my anxiety attack. I was emotionally exhausted and in desperate need of his warm caresses. It reminded my body that it could feel good, too.

But that was done underneath my clothing and the covers.

Each time he's touched me since then, it's been half-clothed for one reason or another.

He hasn't actually seen me naked.

Hasn't discovered the stretch marks, the rolls of skin. And his potential reaction makes me nervous.

Because I've seen him shirtless. Mathias is toned and muscular, not a soft spot on his huge body—the antithesis of mine.

"Don't hide from me," he commands, separating the arms I instinctively crossed to cover myself.

As soon as my breasts are revealed, Mathias dips his head and draws his tongue around a pink areola before sucking the nipple between his lips, the scratch of his perpetual five o'clock shadow doing funny things to my insides.

I latch onto his hair, ruffling the neat strands with my fingertips. "Mathias..." That's as far as my thoughts go.

I should push him away, not pull him closer.

Giving in so easily to his desires doesn't help my cause of leaving the manor and returning to North Carolina by myself.

It only cements that my body loves to ignore my brain and wants to dive into whatever Mathias is offering.

Every. Single. Damn. Time.

"You're not going to come until I say so. Understand, Allie Angel?" His rough fingers rip my panties down my legs before spearing through the damp curls to rub my clit. "And I won't give you permission until I have your complete submission. Ready to convince me, *ma cherie*?"

No.

Yes.

Like a childhood game, the petals of a flower get plucked one by one.

Am I ready to submit? *Yes. No. Yes.*

Is this what I really want? *No. Yes.*

It's a never ending process. The flowers never die. Alway plucking. Never deciding.

Mathias continues his assault on my body. Pinching, licking, stroking. Anything to heighten my arousal and keep me on edge. The more he takes, the more fuzzy my thinking becomes. "Please..." *Please what, Allie? Make a decision. This doesn't have to be hard.*

"If you want to come, then you know what I need to hear," he growls, nipping at my bottom lip. The sting sends a jolt of lightning straight to my pussy, and I know he feels my immediate response by the hum of approval in his throat.

He turns me around and spanks my ass with a swift smack. "That's for hiding those texts from me earlier." *Thwack!* "That's for refusing to give me your phone the first time I asked." *Thwack!* "And that one's just for me, because I love watching your juicy ass jiggle and turn red with my handprint."

His teeth sink into the spot between my neck and shoulder. "Give me what I want. Tell me what I want to hear."

Pluck the petals.

Yes or no?

Yes.

"I... I'm yours," I cry, throwing myself completely into the game. No more hesitation. No matter what comes.

"Not good enough." He buries two fingers deep inside my clenching channel and grinds his palm over my clit.

Moaning, I try again. "I'm sorry for not telling you about Bailey and my family. I'm sorry I tried to handle it myself."

A wave of tears wells to the forefront at the admission, and another realization crystallizes in my mind as shame fights for a place in my ragged emotions. "I fell back into old patterns," I whisper. "That's what got me in this mess in the first place." Another choppy breath. "That's why I need you."

"That's good, baby. What else?" His hot breath is a shock to my skin as he flips me again to suckle the delicate skin of my breasts.

I'm dizzy.

Off-kilter.

Running on pure instinct.

"I'll stop second-guessing you. Us. My decision to give you control." It'll be a relief to let that go. Which I guess is the point.

"That's right," Mathias grunts. His lips shift to hover over mine so our eyes meet, and I see the resolve in his irises. "You submit to me because you trust that I will do what's best for you. Haven't I taken care of you so far? No more secrets, Allie. We need to be honest with each other for this to work, understand?"

"Yes, Mathias."

"Good... Now, come for me like a good girl," he commands.

So, I obey, and finally fly free into the safety of his arms.

CHAPTER TWENTY-FIVE

MATHIAS

The clasp of Allie's hot cunt on my fingers makes my dick jerk for attention. Pre-cum dampens the trapped head straining against my slacks.

She voiced her commitment to our arrangement. *To me.* Without the weight of her terrible roommate or a messy apartment bearing down on her.

"Lay back, but keep your eyes on me," I order as I suck my fingers clean of her sweet cream and unbutton my slacks with the other hand. My shoes get kicked to the side before I fling the rest of my clothing off, too.

Every night, she falls asleep in my bed.

Fully clothed in flimsy pajamas.

And each time, I grit my teeth and restrain the urge to bury my cock in her soft body—all in the name of letting her adjust. I pleasure her with my hands. With my mouth. But we're past that now.

Both naked.

Both hungry for more.

Stroking myself, I allow my gaze to lazily roam over the beautiful pale curves laid before me like a gourmet feast for prisoners on death row.

Allie will be my last meal.

The first woman I've ever claimed for myself.

The last woman I'll ever fuck.

"How sweet you look... My prized little Angel wet and needy for a bastard like me." Her swollen pussy contracts around nothing at the sound of my voice. So responsive. So eager to be stuffed full.

Allie licks her lips while her clouded stare bounces between my thick cock and my face before landing somewhere above my head as a scarlet blush stains her skin from cheeks to cunt.

"I've never..." Her throat works through a nervous swallow. "I've never done this before. Except with a... a dildo," she admits, her voice cracking on the last word.

With her glasses magnifying her pretty blue eyes, she looks even more innocent. A sacrifice to my barbaric cravings.

Satisfaction seeps into my bones. Soothes the feral beast clawing to the surface. The one desperate to pump the innocent pussy before me with its first cock. To drown it in my hot seed.

"Quel plaisir de vous voir... A pure little virgin. My Angel to fuck and debauch."

She whimpers at the promise.

"Tell me, dirty girl, was your dildo as large as me?" Her gaze unerringly finds my cock, my fist wrapped tightly around the base, pointing it directly at her cunt.

"N-No," she stutters.

"Are you sure? Perhaps we should test it." I step closer, notching the head at her entrance before dropping my hands to her hips. The fleshy love handles push between my fingers, and I love the give of her body. It begs me to sink into its warm comforts.

How can I refuse its plea?

The answer is *I fucking can't*. I thrust forward, burying myself deep until my pelvis rubs against her swollen clit.

"Mathias!" Her nails scratch at my arms, the island, anything for purchase.

Rearing back, I plunge forward again, harder.

"Tell me, when you pleasured yourself in the dark of the night, did that measly sex toy stretch your tight little cunt like my fat cock? Did it make you burn? Did it make you drip and soak your mattress?" I ask with filthy curiosity.

I batter in and out of her giving body, each pounding thrust causing a ripple effect on her bountiful curves. Her heavy breasts bouncing. Her belly wobbling. I eat up the view—devouring her with my eyes—and feel a moment of regret for not feasting on her juicy little pussy first.

"No, it didn't... It didn't feel like this. I've never felt like this, Mathias."

Each word sounds like it's pulled from the depths of her, and that's where I want to be, embedded inside the very fabric of Allie's being, owning every single atom of her delicious body and soul.

My sweet little submissive.

Mine. Mine. Mine.

Unbearable pleasure shoots straight to my dick, and with one final thrust, I roar my release, stuffing her full of thick ropes of cum, our combined juices seeping out between us in an obscene display.

"I'm the only man who will ever make you feel this way. You belong to me, Allie Angel." My thumb drops to her clit, and it doesn't take long before she comes again, her orgasm sucking my balls dry.

Using my grip on her hips, I slide her into my arms, and carefully stumble until my back hits the closet wall, and I slip to the floor, cradling her to my chest.

Our hearts beat rapidly as one, our lungs struggling to drag in a full breath. It's harsh, and raw, but euphoric.

Allison is mine, completely, *finally*.

"Tell me about your mother," she whispers, and I stiffen at the unexpected inquiry.

"Why?"

"Because I already know about your father. Because you know so much about me... I feel like you're still a mystery."

Rubbing circles on her back, I consider her question. She has a right to know; I'm not hiding anything from her. But talking about my family puts me in a sour mood, and I'm not ready to lose my peace after coming in her sweet body.

"Please, Mathias."

Fuck. I can't deny her anything, especially when she pleads so softly.

"My mother was a selfish woman. She abandoned me to Conrad once my father ended their arrangement. She washed her hands of us and never looked back. I have no idea where she is, or even if she's still alive."

"I'm sorry," Allie murmurs, kissing my chest, then moving higher to kiss the cross tattoo on my neck. All of the Blackchapel Bastards got them years ago to seal our commitment to each other.

"Don't be. While I hated Conrad and his lessons, one good thing came of it—my brothers."

"You love them."

"They're my family. Not the two people whose DNA I happen to share."

She wiggles closer and sighs. "I'm envious, you know. I wanted to build a strong support system of friends who became family. I thought Bailey would always be there, but I chose poorly."

"Don't say that. You didn't know she'd turn on you. At one point, she treated you well, or else you never would have stayed as loyal as you did. That's an admirable quality, not a weakness." I squeeze her tighter, hating the self-deprecating way she views herself.

"If you say so..." Changing the subject, she mutters, "Tasha's going to have a field day with me tomorrow."

"A lot has happened, but she's equipped to help you through your feelings. And if she's not, then we'll find someone who is."

"I don't want a new therapist, Mathias."

Using my hold on Allie to close the inches of space between us, I grin. "Good, then you'll make it work. Talk about whatever you need to, but keep your involvement with the Blackchapel Bastards vague. All she needs to know is that you're safe and in the care of an extremely handsome man."

Allie playfully punches my arm at that last part, and I grunt from the light impact.

"You're pretty feisty for a woman who just lost her virginity."

"Orgasms give me a second wind," she teases.

"Hmm... Sounds like a challenge to wear you out. Why don't we take a hot bath together?" I hoist her higher in my arms and carefully stand before heading toward the bathroom. "I'll even clean your sore pussy with my tongue."

Allie's laughter is a breath of fresh air. It sweeps away the brutal childhood memories made at Blackchapel Manor and replaces them with joyful ones.

"Such a gentleman."

I turn my head to whisper in her ear. "For you? Always."

CHAPTER TWENTY-SIX

ALLISON

The black screen switches to Tasha as my therapy appointment officially starts the next morning. Squirming in my seat, I search for a comfortable position after having Mathias's weighty cock shunting between my thighs a mere hour ago.

"Hello, Allison, I hope you're well. Let's start with our usual questions. Are you alone?"

I've always appreciated this inquiry.

It sets the boundaries for the session, especially back when Bailey would be in the next room and could possibly hear my venting to Tasha.

"Yes, I'm alone."

"And are you safe?"

Safe.

I think about the myriad of changes in my life lately.

A man swept me away to his decadent mansion, the epicenter for his revenge plot against an international crime group known as The Syndicate, but he also ensured I could keep my current therapist, despite state laws.

He's promised to care for me.

Pushed me to break out of my shell.

Am I safe?

"Yes," I answer with a nod of my head. For the first time, I'm safe in every way—physically, emotionally, and mentally.

"Good. How are you doing?" Tasha relaxes in her ergonomic chair now that she's ascertained I'm okay. "I spoke with your... friend, and he mentioned you moved to Boston?"

Ha! Friend.

Mathias is quite more than such a paltry label. He supports my efforts to find my purpose. He compliments me on my brains *and* my beauty. Which, as the chubby girl known for her smarts, has never even been on my radar.

Is this how people fall in love?

My mouth launches into the story of my whirlwind move to Boston and the new friends I've made—*AKA the Blackchapel Bastards*—but my heart wonders if I'm on the road to happily ever after.

Am I falling in love?

It's at once an exhilarating yet terrifying possibility.

CHAPTER TWENTY-SEVEN

MATHIAS

The lines of account numbers blur as my mind drifts to Allie. She's upstairs in one of the spare bedrooms meeting virtually with her therapist, and I almost wish I'd gone through with my idea of installing a security feed in the room to hear how the session goes. To learn Allie's unfiltered thoughts and feelings. But broaching her privacy in that way seemed a step too far. Especially when she's used to those supposed to care for her, betraying that trust.

So, instead, I lean my head back, stare at the ceiling, and imagine the conversation happening overhead.

"Are Petit's finances boring you?" Luca drawls from his position in the corner of the study. A stack of manila folders rest beside him as he sifts through the older paperwork that Petit hadn't digitized yet.

"It's a tangled web. Outside the legitimate business profits and expenses, the money going toward shell companies bounces around so much, it takes forever to find where it lands."

Maybe I should check on Allie. Make sure the internet connection is strong enough up there. That the video isn't buffering to death.

"It landed." Rafe points over my shoulder where an account in Hong Kong is highlighted in yellow. *Where'd he come from?*

"Looks like SY Shipping is the last stop before Petit transfers funds to his Syndicate buddies." He grabs the mouse and clicks around on the screen. "I recognize this account as one of Sergei Petrov's."

Dmitri and Aleksei's dad.

"We've got him. We have proof Louis Petit funded known criminals dealing in weapons, drugs..." Bracing against the desk, grim relief laces my bones.

Finally.

The first domino in our plan to tear down The Syndicate and our fathers is about to fall. After decades of anger and meticulous preparations.

We no longer need to wait for the perfect moment to strike. The evidence necessary for action is right here.

It's time to make our move.

***

"Do I have to go to this party? It's not like you're really taking over as CEO of Petit Enterprises. You're planning on dismantling the company, right?" Allie asks from her seat on my lap a week later. An episode of the design show she says relaxes her plays in the background.

I playfully swat her ass as the host reveals the couple's remodeled kitchen. "You're my date, *mon petit ange*, so of course, you're coming."

Originally, Petit's death was set in stone. I'd strip his conglomerate to pieces—decimating The Syndicate's major financier, a hefty blow to their organization—then ensure my bastard father ended up buried six feet deep.

But plans change.

Not every father of the Blackchapel Bastards will get off so easily. Some are destined to die at the hands of their son, but Petit will suffer more behind bars.

He wasn't meant to live, but the more I studied him, the more I realized how suffocating a jail cell will be for the flamboyant businessman who loves being the center of attention.

With enough condemning evidence to bring Petit to justice, our plan is now in motion. Starting with the hastily organized party celebrating Blackchapel Inc.'s takeover of Petit Enterprises. Lulling my father into a false sense of safety before our meeting the following day.

I haven't told him what it'll entail, but he won't be leaving without handcuffs clamped around his wrists.

"I don't have anything to wear."

I chuckle at the pout in her tone. "We'll be in Paris. The epicenter of fashion. We'll find you a dress. Now, since you're feeling sassy enough to try defying me, why don't I remind you why I'm in control?"

My lips find hers on a gasp as my hardened cock nudges between her ass cheeks, and thoughts of my father, The Syndicate, and the babbling TV fade to dust in the wake of my Allie Angel.

CHAPTER TWENTY-EIGHT

ALLISON

A cloud of white fills my vision as awareness slowly blinks to life. We arrived in Paris late last night, and despite the private jet housing a comfortable bedroom, I didn't sleep a wink during the flight. *Couldn't.* Not while Mathias and the guys quietly discussed their plan for Louis Petit and his former company.

After years of preparation, the Blackchapel Bastards were finally taking the first step in revenge against their fathers. There'd be no turning back then; they'd have to see it through to the end.

And that has sent my anxiety on a rollercoaster of highs and lows the past two days—from packing for the short trip to imagining how everything could go wrong. Especially since Mathias, Luca, and I were caught in the crosshairs of a drive-by the last time we were in Paris.

I was shot. *Twice.*

Staring out the French doors leading to a balcony, I study the cream-colored exteriors of the buildings lining the street. Mathias chose a small, boutique hotel for our stay, one at the heart of historical Paris rather than near the Petit Enterprises skyscraper. It's a romantic choice I didn't expect from such a practical man.

A warm palm slides up my bare thigh. Stomach. Neck. "What are you thinking so hard about, *ma cherie*?" His thumb frees my bottom lip from where I'd been unconsciously biting it.

"This is an important trip. I'm trying to mentally prepare myself."

He smooths a kiss over my brow as his hand dips to cup my pussy. A wash of heat spreads below my belly at the possessive touch. "Don't dwell on it too much. You'll be safe here while we deal with Petit. For all his faults, Conrad trained us well."

"I'm not worried about myself. I'm worried about you and your brothers. There are seven of you against an international criminal organization. And you're down one man with Aleksei in prison. Those aren't good odds, Mathias."

"Every Syndicate member won't be at the meeting tomorrow," he jokes, beginning to rock his palm against my clit as two fingers tease my opening.

"But they will hear about what goes down, then you'll have targets on your backs. More than you already do."

Mathias rolls so his large body flanks my side, one leg hooking around mine to spread me wider for his handiwork between my thighs. As far as distractions go, being touched by Mathias tops the list, but the slew of concerns weighing on my mind refuses to be thwarted so easily.

"Do you have to meet your father in person? Can't you let Interpol arrest him without first rubbing it in his face that you've won?"

His movements stutter for a second then resume—determination vibrates from his firm caresses and the steeliness in his eyes. "I'm not rubbing anything in his face.

I'm proving to him and myself that I never needed him. That I became a successful force to be reckoned with in the business and criminal realm despite his abandonment."

That sounds like another version of what I said, but I don't call him on it. Mathias made up his mind long before I ever entered his life. All of the Blackchapel Bastards require some sort of closure with their dads.

I just hope closure doesn't cost them.

Permanently.

I don't think any of them could survive losing a brother. *The thought of losing Mathias...* My breath hitches in my lungs, and I quickly slam my eyes shut to avoid him seeing my sudden tears. He's the first person to truly care about my well-being, even more than I do sometimes.

"Enough talk about my father. I want you to come for me, Angel, and then we're taking a town car—with our café crèmes and almond croissants fresh from the *boulangerie*—shopping. You need a gown for this evening."

"But—Mathias!" I gasp and arch my back when he replaces his fingers with his thick cock, the velvety steel plunging deep in one hard thrust.

His lips trace mine before claiming them in a not-so-subtle command to let my fears go. To give them to him.

He's always protecting me, even from myself.

But who will protect him?

***

The Eiffel Tower shines in the distance and sparkling lights decorate the tables and railings. It should be romantic, a dream, yet I'm falling into a nightmare as a prickle of awareness runs beneath my skin.

The first warning sign of an anxiety attack.

Please, not here. Not now.

We're at the company party I tried so hard to get out of, celebrating the new ownership of Petit Enterprises. But this is too much.

Too much pressure.

My hand wraps around the steel railing as I sway forward. My eyes fixate on the long drop below.

Falling would feel like flying.

Flying is freedom.

No! I shake the thought off and clasp the back of Mathias's jacket. It wrinkles under my sweaty palm, but it's my lifeline.

"Mathias," I whisper, urgency infiltrating the one word.

He glances down and must read the distress on my face because he immediately cups the back of my neck, drawing me nearer as a soothing massage begins.

No one else would notice a difference in him because his conversation continues like normal, but I recognize the awareness in his body, the slight protective shift to position himself partially in front of me.

A moment later, Dmitri sidles up to us and easily steers the conversation to a different topic, freeing Mathias to exit the group with me in tow.

The connection the brothers have is unmatched. They don't even have to speak for one to understand they're needed like Dmitri just did. I'm almost jealous of their closeness because I've never felt that with anyone. Least of all, my own brother.

"What's wrong?" Mathias ushers me into an empty hall. "What do you need?"

"Nothing's really wrong," I say, embarrassed by my body's unpredictable reactions. "Tonight is just starting to get to me. I'm so far out of my element here."

And I'm worried about the confrontation planned for tomorrow.

But he's already aware of my feelings where his father is concerned.

That's why he made today so special.

Mathias provided the full *Pretty Woman* treatment after our passionate morning in bed. A band of stylists, a makeup artist, and a hairdresser made me presentable for this evening. The full-length navy gown I found in a luxury boutique on the Champs-Élysées shimmers down my body, and it's the fanciest thing I've ever worn. Hell, this is the fanciest I've ever been.

And it's freaking me out.

I barely recognize the woman in the mirror.

He even got me prescription contacts, so I could skip my glasses for the evening. Though it hasn't stopped me from absentmindedly reaching for my nose to push up the missing frames.

"You're doing great." Mathias hugs me close. "Do I need to provide a distraction?" His hand drifts lower to squeeze my ass, and I chuckle but shake my head.

"No, orgasms can mimic the effects of an attack. Increased heart rate. Tingling sensation. It ends up making things worse. But thanks," I mumble, burying my head in his chest. "Just keep holding me. The feeling should pass soon. It hasn't become a full-fledged attack yet."

"Okay, but first, take this." He removes a flat pill case from his wallet and offers the familiar white tablet.

"How...? When did you start carrying those with you?" I ask in wonder before swallowing the pill. It's my medication for immediate relief from an attack. I can't believe he has them.

"After that first night when I learned about them."

"Thank you."

He cups my face and drops a kiss to my forehead before hugging me again. "Don't thank me for looking after you, Allie. It's my privilege."

We stand silently as I match my breaths to Mathias's even inhales and exhales. I feel bad for distracting him with my problems when we're here as a last *fuck you* before executing the plan for revenge against his dad tomorrow.

When he finally shared what he and his brothers had been searching for all those hours in their office, I was relieved to know it'd come to an end soon.

Although, that just means they'll move on to Luca's dad next since he put out a hit for his illegitimate son.

Such an intricate web.

And dwelling on it isn't going to help your current situation.

Refocusing on my breathing, I slam the door on thoughts about tomorrow but then an anxious voice taunts.

But those aren't the only worries you have...

CHAPTER TWENTY-NINE

MATHIAS

I decide to call it a night once Allie starts feeling better. The rest of the guys can keep up appearances without me. Especially when staying isn't worth Allie's discomfort.

"Let's go back to the hotel. Justin is waiting downstairs in the car," I say, guiding Allie out of the room toward the coat check, despite her protests.

"I'm sorry for cutting things short. You don't have to leave with me."

"I'm not abandoning you. Not when you're so vulnerable. You should know me better than that by now."

Her arms slide through the coat sleeves as I hold it for her before pressing the elevator button. The moment the silver doors close for our descent to the ground floor, she rests her head on my shoulder and sighs.

"I do. I just hate being a burden."

"You're not a burden," I growl, though it's useless to argue when she's so fragile.

Numbered buttons light up for each level we pass until a bell rings and we exit. Justin—a Blackthorn soldier doubling as our driver—waits with our car outside then slips into the driver's seat for the trip to L'Hotel de Marc.

Allie snuggles into my side without another word. City lights flash across her sober features as we journey from Paris La Défense to the 8th arrondissement, both of us contemplating the evening in silence.

Something else is bothering her.

Something she's keeping from me.

And there's no room in our relationship for secrets.

Once we reach our bedroom at the hotel, Allie kicks off her heels and grabs an oversized tee before heading to the bathroom for privacy.

My phone buzzes with a text from Dmitri apprising me of ongoing conversations at the party, but that can wait. There are more important details to discover *here* in this room.

From my woman.

I toss the device aside, and it skips across the bedspread as the bathroom door swings wide to reveal Allie makeup free in a plain sleep shirt. I'm guessing she removed her contacts, too, since she's got this adorable squint going on. The only adornment left from tonight's festivities is the necklace I gave her mere hours ago after a day of shopping.

"Are you sure you're feeling better?" I ask, needing to reassure myself that she's well enough to consent to this next part.

"Yeah, between the pill and you, it's like it never happened. Thank god." She hangs the silky gown she was wearing in the closet and smooths a hand down the shimmering fabric.

I shrug off my jacket and undo the first few buttons of my shirt before sitting on the edge of the bed. Resting my forearms on my knees, I allow myself to dive into a different headspace. One prepared to properly care for my woman's needs—even the unconscious ones she's only vaguely aware of.

"Good," I murmur, low and possessive. "Crawl for me."

"What?" Allie jolts in surprise. Her blue eyes flash with interest before questions cloud her instinctive response. "Why?"

"Because I asked you to, and you love obeying me. Like a good girl should."

She doesn't argue with my assessment, instead, her knees bend slowly until she's kneeling on the carpet and her fingertips flex against the thick fabric, a shuddering sigh filling the air.

A man less attuned to Allie's every breath might have missed the soft relief of her exhale.

But not me.

Some men might punish her for voicing a question. See it as a brat's way of asserting control. But I know my little Angel.

She needs solid boundaries. Concrete points to understand the mysteries of the world around her. That's why she stayed stuck in terrible situations for so long. She knew what to expect from them.

In a way, they were safe.

The brain is a complex organ with a vast number of pathways, and Allie's unique mind requires the reassurance I can give. Once she has it, she submits beautifully. Willingly.

My sweet, innocent girl.

I'll never take her trust for granted.

When Allie is close enough, I insert a finger through the dangling heart hidden between her breasts. The gifted necklace is made of delicate gold chain links with two heart outlines at the ends. Worn normally, the hearts loop together, allowing one to drop lower into a woman's cleavage.

But the best part is when they come into play, like now, as I gently pull on one heart, forcing its twin to slide higher on the chain until the necklace becomes a choker around Allie's neck. Tugging her closer, I pat the inside of my thigh in encouragement, and she complies by lowering her cheek to the hard muscle.

"I didn't say anything earlier, but you were worried about something before the overwhelm of the party. What's bothering you, *ma cherie*? Tell me what it is, so I can fix it."

She's been reserved all evening. At the party, I chalked it up to being surrounded by strangers, but even on the flight yesterday, Allie was huddled within herself. Refusing to rest.

Her lashes flutter closed as she licks her lips. "You already know my feelings about tomorrow. This isn't about that," she begins. Then stops. Her nose scrunches like she's fighting an internal war. "If I start taking care of myself again, does that mean you'll stop? Like if I miraculously get one hundred percent healthy?"

The soft question sends a crack through my stone cold heart.

"No, sweetheart. That's what we're working towards. To you feeling healthy enough emotionally and mentally to handle independent tasks while understanding that your care doesn't rely entirely on you. I *want* you at one hundred percent because you're a damn force to be reckoned with," I remind her. "I'm here, and I will ensure you're taken care of even when you can't. You've proven for a long time how capable you are. Our relationship isn't meant to discredit that. I'm not caring for you because you're too weak to do it yourself. I'm doing it because I want to. Plain and simple. Because I *need* to."

A sigh of relief warms my leg and causes my cock to jump at the brief heat. Her pretty mouth is so close, but as much as I'd love having her plump lips wrapped around my dick, now isn't the time.

This is about *her* needs.

What's best for my Allie Angel will always be priority.

"After tomorrow, we're heading to my chateau in Nice." My hand tenderly strokes her loose curls, massaging her scalp as I relay the upcoming plan. I'll confront Louis Petit in the morning then be on the road for a relaxing vacation with my girl by the afternoon.

If everything goes smoothly.

"Why? I figured we'd immediately head home to start work on Luca's father."

An amused chuckle rumbles in my chest. My little revenge seeker. She fits in so well with me and the rest of the Blackchapel Bastards.

"Because we both need a break," I say. "Though you've been away from Bailey and your family, you've been surrounded by the tension at the manor as we worked to build a case against my father. That ends tomorrow. We'll relax for a few weeks, enjoy the peace of the chateau, before flying back to Boston to deal with Enzo D'Amora."

Allie nuzzles deeper into my thigh and hums in agreement. Contentment sweeps across her cheeks as I continue my gentle stroking, lulling her into a peaceful headspace.

"Sounds perfect," she murmurs.

Yes, it will be.

Time passes slowly in our secluded bubble. Marked by the rhythmic sweep of the Eiffel Tower's beacon across the walls and windows.

Eventually, her head lifts from my lap, and she slides her palm up my leg, slowly reaching for the clasp of my trousers.

Covering her smaller hand with mine, I shake my head. "You don't have to do that, baby."

"Please... I want to."

How can I deny her?

I let go, and Allie carefully slips the button loose and pulls down the zipper before wrestling my cock free. Cherry lips circle the tip and gently suck, her head returning to its place on my thigh as she begins a leisurely rhythm.

Caressing her hair, I shudder at the sight of her tender submission. She's so beautiful—whether it's in a haute couture gown for the party or nothing but a tee like now—my woman is gorgeous from the inside out.

She gives and gives, never expecting anything in return, but I plan on granting her every desire.

Always.

CHAPTER THIRTY

ALLISON

There's something soothing about sucking Mathias's cock. The wide girth stretches my lips, and when the large head bumps the back of my throat, tears rise to the surface. By all accounts, it shouldn't bring comfort.

Yet it does.

"You're doing so well, *mon petit ange*." The low timbre of his voice is a lullaby I could listen to on repeat. Deep and gravelly, it drowns out the static of my thoughts.

His thumb wipes away a stray tear, and I watch as he licks the salty droplet, moaning at the sensual act and causing his cock to pulse in my mouth. More pre-cum coats my tongue. The clean, male taste of him an aphrodisiac.

Increasing the hard pulls of my mouth, I cup his heavy balls and massage their velvety firmness. His muscles tense beneath my cheek, and I know he won't last much longer.

My strong, controlled man except when it comes to me. I may never totally understand what I fulfill inside Mathias, but I know it's important. Vital. I hold as much power over him as he does over me.

Mathias grips the back of my head and groans as the first hot splashes of his release hit the back of my throat. I swallow what I can... until we reverse positions.

The ceiling barely blinks into view before a tongue lashes my clit, Mathias intent on evening the score with his face buried between my thighs.

"W-What are you doing?" I gasp, arching into his ravenous mouth.

His lips wrap around my clit and suck, refusing to accept anything less than my complete and utter destruction as an unexpected orgasm bursts to life.

"Isn't it obvious? I'm fucking my woman." He abandons his position of licking me through the climax in favor of notching his dick to my entrance and shoving deep. Plunging through my clenching channel with brutal force.

"Mathias!" Black teases the edges of my vision as his fierce gaze bores into mine. His fingers pluck and pinch my nipples through the shirt, and instinctively, I wiggle to tear it off, giving him free access to every part of my body. Something he quickly takes advantage of with a bite to my nipple.

A growled "You're mine" rumbles over my heart as he thrusts forward, his pelvis rubbing my clit. "Say it."

"I'm yours," I rasp, emotion clogging my throat.

Mathias kisses my cheek. My forehead. Whispers promises.

"I will always take care of you." A shiver that has nothing to do with his powerful cock wracks my body. "You are safe." Tears well in my eyes. "You are my sweet, beautiful Allie Angel, and I will always protect you. You are so precious to me."

The dam breaks, and as another orgasm roars to life, years of brittle independence shatter from the strength of Mathias's devotion.

And I cry.

Deep, heaving sobs while pleasure sweeps through every cell.

Mathias grunts, wet heat spilling between us, before he collapses on his side and holds me close, a sense of security patching the cracks in my heart.

"I'm here," he murmurs, rubbing circles on my back. "Breathe, baby. I'm here. I will never abandon you."

I'm falling in love with you.

***

The hotel suite is quiet with the men gone. Their meeting with Petit started ten minutes ago, which is right around the time the knot in my belly grew into full-blown nausea, although Mathias assured me that he'd be safe.

That all of them would be.

Including me.

Because he left a security detail behind to watch over me. I'm guessing they're hanging out in the hall. Bored out of their minds with babysitting duty.

"Let's see what French television has to offer," I mutter. Talking to myself relieves the quiet tomb-like quality that's fallen over the room.

A morning show appears, and I let it run in the background, happy for the cheerful noise.

Mathias and his brothers are meeting with his father in a conference room at Petit Enterprises, and I can't shake the worry slinking down my spine. I don't care how careful Mathias is. He can't actually control everything.

From what I've learned of The Syndicate, they're not going to let one of their own go down without a fight. Mathias and Blackchapel Inc. may have purchased Petit Enterprises fair and square, but they can't expect to expose Petit's illegal financial schemes without consequences.

What those will be has me on edge.

When a commercial starts, I mindlessly flip through TV channels of French shows, until a knock on the hotel door jerks me out of my daze. The clock on the TV guide shows it's 10:15 A.M. Too early for lunch from room service. Maybe it's housekeeping?

Or one of the security guys checking on me? Although they're usually pretty discreet.

Preparing myself for an awkward conversation in French, I swing the door open only to be surprised by two masked strangers. The men who were supposed to protect me lay slumped on the floor.

Oh, shit.

Mathias is going to kill me for not checking the peephole. That is, if these guys don't kill me first.

My body freezes in shock, a terrified scream trapped in my throat.

"*Attrape-la!*"

I barely block one of the men as he shoves me into the door frame. His friend quickly follows with an uncapped needle in his hand, and pure fear sends adrenaline pumping through my veins.

I can't breathe.

My chest hurts.

Am I having a heart attack?

I want to kick and shout and cry for Mathias, but the moment I attempt to call for help, the prick of a needle slides into my neck.

For a second, everything is crystal clear and in slow motion—my kidnappers hauling me undetected into the emergency stairwell, being thrown in the trunk of a maroon car.

Then, everything goes dark.

CHAPTER THIRTY-ONE

MATHIAS

"This bastard deserves what's coming to him," Luca mutters, checking his watch for the third time. Petit and his cronies are late, and it's pissing us off.

"Sir," Nathaniel, the head of our security detail for the meeting, approaches with a tablet. "We have confirmation that Petit is here and in the elevator, but there's been a development." He turns the tablet my way to reveal Petit, a contingent of bodyguards, and a familiar woman in the middle of them, leaning heavily on one guard.

"What the fuck? How the hell did he get Allison?"

"Shit!" Luca bangs his fist against the table as Jonah straightens in his seat.

"Looks like two men drugged her guards' breakfast and knocked on her door. She opened it without issue, which is when they injected a paralytic."

The screen switches to play a video from the hotel's security camera aimed at the suite we share. Two men in black. Allie opening the door without hesitation. The hired thugs barging through to shove a needle in her neck.

When she's safe in my arms again, I'm going to redden her ass for not checking the peephole... again. Just like our first meeting at her apartment.

I turn away from the video.

I can't watch any more or the calm demeanor I need to deal with Petit and save Allison will be completely unreachable. Fuck, fuck, *fuck*.

My renowned composure has never been more necessary, yet I feel it cracking with each second Allie's not safe in my arms.

The ding of the elevator rings through the air, signaling Petit's arrival. Forcing a nonchalant, stony facade, I nod and wave Nathaniel back.

This cordial meeting is about to get a whole lot bloodier. Good thing we cleared the building in preparation for today. We didn't want civilian employees caught in potential crossfire, and I'm glad I did one thing right today.

Because I failed to protect Allie.

"*Bonjour*, Mathias." Petit grins as he saunters into the room with Allie in tow. *God, she looks so vulnerable between those two meatheads he has manhandling her.*

He thinks he has the upper hand, but it's only a matter of time before we turn the tables on him. I just have to figure out how before Allie becomes collateral damage.

"Father," I say smoothly. I refuse to give him the satisfaction of knowing he surprised me.

"You've been busy lately. Too busy to introduce your paramour, hmm?" Petit gestures to Allie. She's groggy as one of his men roughly pushes her into a leather seat, forcing me to bite my tongue hard enough to bleed to prevent a growl of warning.

"This is a business meeting, not a social call. Should I have brought Denise or Veronica?" The mention of my father's two mistresses causes a boom of laughter.

"Those women are a dime a dozen as you Americans would say. But this one..." He jerks Allie's chin his way. "She matters to you, doesn't she, son? You've installed her in Conrad's old manor like a proper wife."

"I would think you'd appreciate the ease of having a woman at your beck and call. Ms. Field's presence suits until I find someone else who interests me," I lie. I'm never giving Allie up, but all I can do is fake disinterest in the hope that Petit believes me.

"You're lying."

"And you're boring me," Luca interjects. He tosses several folders on the table. "These reports outline how you've been siphoning money for The Syndicate into various illegal avenues. Copies have been sent to Interpol, who should be on their way as we speak."

"You think I'm going to prison?" Another bark of humor rises from Petit. It's getting on my fucking nerves how amused he finds this.

Let him laugh.

All the way to fucking jail.

"We know you are. You're done, Petit," Jonah says. "With your criminal dealings exposed, The Syndicate can't risk protecting you."

"You boys really think you have everything figured out, don't you? Conrad filled your heads with nonsense about revenge as if children can dismantle a century's old establishment."

The elevator bell rings again. "Ah, that will be Sergei. I'm sure he took care of the poor Interpol agents sent to apprehend me."

Sergei Petrov, Dmitri and Aleksei's father and notorious arms dealer, stepped out of the elevator with a swath of men armed to the teeth.

Goddammit! Our last bit of intel said Sergei was home in Russia. Somehow he slipped Dmitri's surveillance.

"Louis, why am I always cleaning up your messes?" Sergei drawls with a heavy Russian accent as he studies the room. "I see my son didn't come with you three. Too bad. I would've liked to see him."

He shrugs before raising his gun and shooting the Blackthorn guard next to Nathaniel. The man's body drops dead to the carpet, and all hell breaks loose as everyone ducks for cover while pulling out their own weapons.

I scramble to Allison's side and pull her to the floor under the table. "Allie? Stay with me, baby. I'm getting you out of here."

We crawl down the length of the table toward the door leading to a supply closet. Last night, Jonah and Luca cut an escape route through the side wall, and I've never been so glad for plotting a hundred ways how something can go wrong and finding solutions to every single contingency.

Except for Allie being captured and drugged.

My failure weighs on me, but dwelling on it now won't do me any good. Luca and Jonah already have the closet door open, shooting decisively at Sergei and Petit's men.

"Thank fuck for that paranoid mind of yours," Luca shouts, pushing Jonah down as a bullet explodes in the wall where his head used to be.

"Thank me later. Let's kill these sons of bitches and get out of here. I preferred plan B anyway." Plan A was Interpol and going the legal route for retribution. Plan B is the 'fuck it, let's just kill him' solution.

Except someone already beat me to it because my father is crumpled on the ground with blood seeping out of a hole in his forehead. Of course the fucker robbed me of my chance to finish him off.

"Damn, which one of you killed him?"

"I think it was a stray bullet. Sorry, brother. Take your girl and get out of here. We've got this. Nathaniel and his guys are helping us finish off who is left. Sergei already fucking left."

"More slippery than a snake," Jonah mutters.

Annoyance flares in my gut, but dead is dead. Petit is finally out of my life permanently. Later, maybe I'll examine how that makes me feel after decades of loathing the man. Or maybe I'll just drink a tumbler of Scotch and call it a day.

"We'll get Sergei. We'll get all of them," I promise while covering Allie's head and ushering her into the supply closet.

I remove the shelving unit covering the large hole cut into the drywall, and a few minutes later, we crouch and shuffle through the opening into the hallway.

"Come on, Allie. Just a little further to go."

"I knew... you'd save... me," she heaves, holding a hand to her stomach.

"Don't try to talk yet. You're still fighting the drug they injected." We hurry toward the emergency exit stairs. Our heavy breathing drowned out by the firestorm happening behind us. "Soon, you'll be safe. A doctor will check—"

"Mathias!"

Worried that a stray bullet hit her, I turn to throw my body on hers, but she's already crashing into me amidst a gunshot blast. A grunt of pain whooshes from her lips, and immediately, I raise my weapon and kill the bastard who appeared at the end of the hall to block our escape.

The worst sort of familiarity descends as I roll over and cradle her head above the hard floor. Our positions mirror the fateful February morning when we met, and helpless rage pours through my veins.

Not again.

Why do I keep failing her?

CHAPTER THIRTY-TWO

ALLISON

I never wanted to get shot again.

But when the man with a raised gun peeked out from behind a cubicle wall, instinct took over, and I moved between Mathias and a bullet.

Like a magnet drawn to repel danger.

The only saving grace is this time I know I didn't do it because I wanted to die.

I want to live.

I want to be with Mathias.

It just sucks that it may not happen.

Mathias gently lowers me to the floor, a panicked edge entering his voice. "Fuck, baby. Why the hell did you step in front of me?"

Now is as good a time as ever to admit it, I suppose. To let go of my last fear. To share my final secret. Who knows if I'll get another chance?

"Because I... love... you."

His hand circles my throat where I'm still wearing the heart necklace he gave me. "*Je t'aime, mon petit ange.* You don't get to die. I forbid it. You can't leave. Not after you tore my heart out of my chest and made it your own. You hear me, *mon amour*? You have to live because I'm not done loving you."

Only Mathias would think he could control this and forbid me to die. I try laughing, but end up coughing instead. Blood splatters onto my glasses.

That can't be good.

"Stay with me." Mathias's lips press harshly into mine. Bet he can taste the copper of my blood on his tongue. "*Reste avec moi, s'il te plaît, ma douce. Je t'aime.*"

Warmth seeps into my bones as everything becomes fuzzy. My heart slows and a calmness settles over me. All those times I secretly wished to die. Wished my pain would end. And now when I find happiness, my wish is granted.

It's not fair.

But I always knew I wasn't meant for a happily ever after.

CHAPTER THIRTY-THREE

MATHIAS

She died.

Allison's heart stopped beating. Her lungs stopped breathing. She died right in my arms.

And took my entire soul with her.

"Come on, brother. We've got to get her to a hospital." Luca hefts Allie's limp weight into his arms while Jonah urges me to stand. The four of us rush down the stairs to the black SUV where Hugo has been waiting.

"What the hell happened?" he shouts, eyes widening after glimpsing Allie's pale, unmoving form. "Oh, shit. Hang on."

The squeal of the tires barely penetrates my fog as Luca carefully lets Allie's head rest in my lap. *My sweet Angel.* He's performing CPR to keep her blood pumping, and every once in a while he instructs me to breathe for her.

Hell, I'd die for her if I could.

I'd take her place in a second.

But life doesn't work that way.

Especially not for a Blackchapel Bastard.

***

"Do it," I order, standing impatiently in front of the brick wall in an abandoned alley hours later.

"You're crazy. I'm not shooting you."

"If you don't, I'll force someone from Blackthorn to do it. You know I will," I warn Luca. He and the rest of my brothers are huddled ten feet from me, bracing against the icy rain falling from the sky.

Allison is still in the ICU, but the doctors are hopeful for a full recovery. After they revived her in the emergency room, she was rushed to surgery to repair damage from the bullet. It's been an agonizing six hours, but the pain isn't over yet.

My girl has stepped between me and a bullet too many times.

It's time to even the score. To know the pain she put herself through. To show her how much she matters to me.

What hurts her, hurts me.

We're bonded for life.

"Fine, I'll do it." Dmitri steps forward, lifts his gun with a silencer attached to the end, and fires three shots to match the three bullets Allie sustained. First from the drive-by, then from the incident this morning. "Crazy motherfucker."

I grunt but remain standing, reveling in the blaze of fire arcing through my body. The doctors are going to have a field day treating me when I lie about a mugging gone wrong and my wounds match the exact placement of my girl's.

But *c'est la vie*.

I'll do anything for my woman.

Even share the pain of bullets meant for me.

CHAPTER THIRTY-FOUR

ALLISON

A sense of déjà vu hits me like a sledgehammer to the head. The beeping machines. My body aching. And the foreboding presence of a shadowy man in the corner.

"M-Mathias?" His name is a croak from my dry throat, a garbled mess, but the swift intake of breath lets me know that he heard me just fine.

"Allie... Thank fuck, you're awake." He slides his chair across the linoleum until he's so close, his knees bump the bed as he rests his elbows on the edge of the mattress, distress emanating from his tense muscles. Along with an IV connected to his arm.

Alarm dispels my haziness. "What happened? How'd you get hurt?" I groan from lifting my hand to gently touch the sling on his arm. It's reminiscent of the one I had to wear after my first gunshot wounds.

Wow. Never thought I'd need to make that distinction—my first, second, and third bullet injuries.

"It's nothing. Tell me how you're feeling. You've been asleep for two days," he says, his voice grittier than usual. Has he been here this whole time? His hair's askew, his clothes wrinkled.

A bit of plastic pops out of the top of his shirt pocket, and my brow furrows at the jade color.

The shade reminds me of the frames I bought special months ago in the hopes that the fun color would spice up my everyday wardrobe. Then they promptly disappeared after my first hospital stay in France.

Plucking the item from Mathias's pocket, I catch a glimpse of blood spatter on the edges of the lenses before his hand covers mine.

"What... Why do you have my glasses? My *old* glasses?"

Voices from the hall filter into the room, and I think I recognize Luca and Jonah's low murmurs mixed in, but the wave of relief I feel knowing they're okay is nothing compared to the intense curiosity burning through me now.

Mathias removes the glasses from his pocket and slowly examines them, his silver gaze softening. "I had to remove them when we first met. They were blocking me from seeing your eyes clearly, since they were dotted with rain and blood. And now... I like keeping them close as a reminder of my promise to you and how I've failed in the past."

"You haven't failed—"

"You took a bullet for me, Allie. *Again*. And this time you almost died. You *did* die. In my arms. For the longest minutes of my life." His pallor pales as his eyes close at the painful memory. "You are mine to protect. *Always*. Yet I've never felt as useless as I have around you. What kind of man gets his woman shot multiple times?"

The agony in his voice breaks my heart. "You can't control everything, Mathias. Accidents happen. Choices are made. I chose to save you from harm both times, and you would do the same if the roles were reversed. If you saw the gunman first, if we were positioned differently. You can't blame yourself for something neither of us could have predicted."

My strong protector.

He doesn't even realize how much he's rescued me from—mentally, emotionally. Things that don't heal as easily or naturally as bullet wounds. Things not as visible or tangible but arguably more damaging.

Cupping his bearded cheek, I wait until his eyes meet mine before sharing that truth, desperate to impress upon him how much he's done for me.

"Don't ever think you've failed me. You protected me from Bailey. From my family. People who were supposed to love and support me. It took a dangerous stranger—*you*—to drag me from the depths of my depression and help me breathe again. To free me."

Tears spill down my cheeks as I try to hold myself together long enough to finish. Like lancing a wound, I need to let everything out. Need to let him know how I feel.

"I would take a thousand bullets for you, Mathias. Not because of what you've done for me. Or what you'll do in the future. But because I love you."

"Fuck, baby." He hunches forward to press a hard kiss to my lips, but before we can go too much further, he jerks back with a hiss and shakes the tubing of his IV. "Damn inconvenient—"

"You never told me why you're hooked up to that thing."

"As part of my vow to keep you safe and penance for failing—" he holds a hand up to stop my rebuttal since we just covered that—"I asked Dmitri to give me matching bullet wounds to yours."

"You... What?" Shock courses down my spine as I study the sling on his arm with new light. "How are you here with me? You should be in bed recovering. Three bullet wounds! Are you insane?"

I can't believe his crazy brothers agreed to his ridiculous plan. He must be in more pain than he's letting on, too, because I don't feel great, and I'm only dealing with one injury.

Then there's my own insane heart that thinks it's kind of sweet that he'd go to such extreme lengths to prove his loyalty and love. Even though he's shown me countless times.

Mathias scoffs. "I'm fine. I have a strong constitution, and the doctors know where to find me if things go south." His fingers intertwined with mine. "I'm not being separated from you again. The hours they kept me holed up in another room without knowing how you were doing was torture."

"Have them bring a second bed in here, then—"

"Knock, knock. Who's up for visitors?" Luca pokes his head through the door while Rafe, Jonah, Hugo, and Dmitri hang back in a huddle full of flowers and balloons. I even spy a teddy bear hoisted in Hugo's large arms.

"How are you doing? You scared us back there," Luca says after I motion for everyone to enter.

"I've been better. The same can't be said for you guys. What were you thinking shooting Mathias?"

A round of groans rises from the group as they turn to Dmitri. He raises his hands and shakes his head. "I was just following orders. I can't help it if your man has wild ideas on how to prove his devotion."

"Just wait until your woman shows up..." Mathias growls under his breath, but a smile hides in the corners of his mouth.

"Well, in the future, I'd appreciate it if you refused any outlandish requests. He can take it up with me, if he disagrees." Mathias licks his lips and spares a glance at his brothers before leaning forward, careful of his IV this time, and whispers in my ear. "Topping from the bottom, Angel?"

A shiver of heat sends a blush to my cheeks as my heart squeezes in time with his heavy breaths. Mathias knows I enjoy his dominant tendencies, whether it's in the bedroom or not, but I've also learned that I hold more power than I thought.

He wants what's best for me. Cares about my needs. Which means I get what I want. Especially if that's his brothers never shooting, stabbing, or whatever else kind of nonsense Mathias orders in an attempt to prove something to me.

Because he loves me.

CHAPTER THIRTY-FIVE

ALLISON

As soon as we're able to travel, Mathias packs me into the private jet, and we fly back to Boston where he hasn't left my side. It's sweet and should feel overbearing, but I love being the center of his attention.

The only downside is our little vacation to Nice got postponed, since he wants me to recover in our home.

Oh, and the fact that we have matching scars. How can I forget that?

"I've got something for you," Mathias says as he returns to my side in the library with a mug of tea.

"I see that." I make a *gimme* motion with my hands, and he carefully hands over the mug with a sly smile.

"Not that. *This*." A square box appears from behind his back.

Temporarily setting aside my drink, I study the gift as my fingertips smooth along the velvet casing. I'm not usually a jewelry-wearing girl, but for Mathias, I'd do just about anything.

And this looks like the *best* kind of jewelry.

"Go on," he instructs, and I pop the box open to reveal a diamond ring with tinier diamonds decorating the band.

Mathias plucks the stunning ring from its black bedding and kneels on one knee in front of me.

"This is a symbol of our relationship. Of our commitment to each other. I want to marry you, and if you accept my ring, you're giving me your promise of forever. This isn't about keeping you chained. It's about providing you freedom to be everything you can be. Safely. Without fear. Because you know I'll be right beside you. Because I love you. Will you be my wife, Allie Angel?"

Smiling, tears spill down my cheeks.

"Yes, I will." I present my hand to Mathias, and the cool metal slides onto my finger, a perfect fit. A sense of security wraps around me like a cozy blanket.

This is where I'm meant to be—in Boston with Mathias, even with his dangerous vendetta against The Syndicate.

So, I guess the City of Lights *did* change my life for the better. And Audrey Hepburn's Sabrina wasn't the only girl to find love after Paris.

I did, too.

My whispered desire came true.

***

Love epilogues? Check out Mathias and Allie's here[1] for a peek into their future together!

---

1. https://bookhip.com/MKDPBBQ

PROLOGUE

LUCA D'AMORA

SEVEN YEARS OLD

"Papa, I don't want to stay here," I say for the fifth time. My father, Enzo D'Amora, ignores me and uses the elaborate door handle to announce our arrival at the manor. Green ivy climbs the brick walls of the massive structure, and I'm reminded of Mama's favorite book *The Secret Garden*. I wonder if there is one hiding around here.

"You don't have a choice, son. With your mama gone, this is the best place for you." Enzo has explained this multiple times, but I still don't understand why I must lose my papa and mama within the same week.

"I'm your son. I should live with you." My arms stubbornly cross my chest as I glare at the huge oak door that swings open. A man and a boy my age stand in the entry to greet us.

"Enzo," the man clips, offering his hand to my father. They nod in greeting before Enzo tells me to go with the boy while he stays to discuss arrangements with Conrad, the manor owner.

"Hugo will show you to your new room. Remember to behave," Papa warns.

"Listen to your father," Conrad adds. "Blackchapel Manor is your home now. Don't disrespect it or me."

Hugo grabs my arm and tugs me toward the massive staircase while muttering under his breath, "Come on. I'll introduce you to Mathias and Jonah."

There are more boys?

Suddenly, this feels more like an orphanage for the unwanted than a safe haven while Papa figures out what to do with me.

I know he loves me.

He and Mama said so.

But he's also part of the Italian mafia and is married to the don's daughter. Papa can't have a bastard son living with his wife and newborn son—my half-brother.

That's what I overheard him tell Mama the day before she succumbed to her illness.

So, I need to live at Blackchapel Manor with his old friend Conrad Steele until he can figure out other arrangements.

But I'm starting to wonder if Papa will come back for me at all...

***

Continue reading Luca and Eden's story in *Broken Innocence*!

THANKS FOR READING & DON'T FORGET TO RATE/ REVIEW!

Please consider leaving a rating/review. Ratings & reviews are the #1 way to support an indie author like me.
The more reviews, the more my books are shown to other potential readers!
And they serve as guides to readers on whether or not to take a chance on an indie author.
I appreciate your support!
XO, Hallie

ABOUT THE AUTHOR

Hallie prefers steamy, insta-love stories where curvy girls are claimed by filthy-talking heroes. And when she ran out of reading material, she decided to write her own stories. If you want a quick, hot read, she's your girl!

Don't miss out on Hallie Bennett updates by joining her VIPs[1]!

---

1. https://www.thearrowedheart.com/hallie-bennett

www.ingramcontent.com/pod-product-compliance
Lightning Source LLC
Chambersburg PA
CBHW022144240626
47153CB00007B/2496